BIRCHING HIS BRIDE

BOOK 1 IN THE DOMESTIC DISCIPLINE SERIES

GOLDEN ANGEL

Cover art by DesignRans

Edited by MJ Edits

Formatted by Raisa Greywood

Thank you so much for picking up my book!

Would you like to receive two free romances from me as well? Join the Angel Legion and sign up for my newsletter! You'll immediately receive a free Stronghold Doms holiday story from the Stronghold in a welcome message as well as a link to pick up book 1.5 of my Bridal Discipline series!

As part of the Angel Legion you'll also receive one newsletter a month with teasers, sneak peeks, news about upcoming releases, and well as what I'm reading now.

ACKNOWLEDGMENTS

Thank you so much to all my fans who continue to support my writing endeavors.

A huge thank you to AquaPrincess who helped me shape this new story, it wouldn't be what it is without you.

Thank you to Lee Savino, my author sensei.

And, as always, thank you to my husband who is ever supportive and delightful.

PROLOGUE

*E*dwin Villiers, also known as Lord Hyde, was about to witness his first female birching. It was a highly anticipated event, for although the young man was quite familiar with the birch from his school days, he hadn't realized such harsh methods could be used on the more delicate, feminine sex. During his school days, he'd gotten into quite a few scrapes with his two best friends, Wesley Spencer, now Earl of Spencer and Hugh Stanley, whose title was Viscount Petersham. When they'd met, they were all sons of earls, destined for positions of wealth and power and had indulged in the usual wild antics of the masculine rakish aristocracy. All good looking and charming young men in their early twenties, they had a bit of experience with the feminine sex, but both Wesley and Edwin had been astonished to learn that their good friend Hugh Stanley, Viscount Petersham, had experience in an area they were entirely unfamiliar with—feminine discipline.

It was not unusual for brothers to watch their sisters being punished, in fact, it was quite often a young boy's first glimpse at a female's rounded bottom, even if he was in no position to be appreciative of the sight. However, unlike Hugh, Edwin and Wesley did not possess sisters and they hadn't realized young girls and ladies might be punished in the same way they and their brothers had. Edwin was an only child and Wesley had three young brothers but not a single sister. When Hugh had begun telling them stories about his father's recent attempts to bring his sister, Eleanor, to heel (as she had become rather spoiled and willful under their mother's care) they'd scarcely believed him.

Petersham's father, the Earl of Harrington, was a strict taskmaster, although less so with his son and heir than with his spoiled brat of a daughter, Eleanor. After all, young men were expected to sow their wild oats and Hugh had never done anything worse than most of his peers, certainly he didn't have the reputation of a complete reprobate. Eleanor, on the other hand, was enough to make a father despair.

At eighteen years of age, the young beauty should have been already presented to Society, but her father had decided she needed an extra year of polish. In truth, he had recently discovered his wife had overindulged the girl to the point of ridiculousness and now Eleanor was determined to get her own way in all things, whether or not what she wanted was right or reasonable. She and her mother had been living on their own in the family's house in Brighton for most of the past six years while Harrington had attended to his business in London and done what he could to raise his heir. Although he had visited numerous times, it wasn't until he'd spent a full summer in the company of his wife and daughter, in preparation for her debut, that he'd realized just how out of hand the situation had become and had made the decision to step in and fulfill his neglected parental duties to his daughter.

Of course, he didn't blame her for her wild ways, he knew it was his wife's indulgence which had created Eleanor's attitude, but he was quite determined to correct it. Hugh's friends had been astonished to learn his father birched Eleanor as part of his corrective measures, his quest to curb her in the shortest amount time possible so she could be presented without dishonoring the family. They'd been even more taken aback to discover Hugh had played witness to these birchings on more than one occasion, his father deeming it necessary for him to learn how to tame a wayward woman. Surprised by their interest, but acknowledging they too might benefit from such instruction, Hugh had offered to share this intriguing sight with his friends, the next time they were on location when there was to be a spanking or birching. Of course, they had immediately agreed.

Now, finally, it was happening. They had come to Brighton with Hugh to visit his family, and at first their presence had ensured Eleanor's good behavior as she'd been distracted by the presence of young, attractive men other than her brother in the house. When she was younger she had followed them around relentlessly, now Wesley and Edwin were doing their own following of her and her friends (much to Hugh's amusement and resignation). But Eleanor had been bucking her father's decrees on matter of dress for months now and it had only been a matter of time before she rebelled.

Today Edwin, Hugh and Wesley had been escorting Eleanor and her friends through some shops when Lord Harrington had happened upon them and seen Eleanor had snuck out of the house in a dress he had already deemed inappropriate for day wear. Truly, the neckline was too low cut for a morning outing, although, of course, none of the gentlemen remarked on it. Seeing the hint of Eleanor's splendid bosom was not something Edwin nor Wesley objected to, and her brother could be understandably excused for not noticing his sister's décolletage, as he was more focused on the other young ladies accompanying her. However, her father was enraged at this immodest sight and had immediately demanded Eleanor's return home, promising her she would be soundly disciplined.

Recognizing his father's turn of phrase, Hugh had immediately asked his friends if they wished to accompany him and see the promised sight. To which, of course, they had quickly agreed.

Now Edwin, Hugh, and Wesley were quietly tucked into the gallery above Lord Harrington's study, watching him lecture Eleanor.

"Are you sure he's going to do it?" asked Edwin. In all his twenty-four years he'd never thought he'd see a sight such as Hugh promised, and he wasn't entirely sure it was going to be forthcoming today. He couldn't imagine such a thing, especially not with a virginal young beauty like Eleanor. All three men were quite successful with women, but they confined their activities to widows, the bored married ladies of the *ton* and the occasional ladybird. He had to admit to himself that he was quite as excited about seeing young Eleanor's untouched body as he was of the promised birching. Although he'd known her when she was younger, the older version of Eleanor was much more attractive to him with her honey blonde hair and sparkling blue eyes that looked at him so haughtily. She had the kind of icy exterior that made a man want to see what he could coax from beneath it.

"Absolutely," Hugh whispered back, his voice confident. "He's just making her squirm. He says anticipation makes the lesson stick better."

"Then why does she keep defying him?" asked Wesley, also keeping his voice low. Hugh had assured them he didn't think his father would care about an audience, but as he did not have actual permission, they were taking care not to be heard. "You'd think being birched would make a woman think twice about her actions. God knows I did everything I could to avoid it."

"Except actually behaving," Edwin muttered.

Hugh shrugged. "That's just Nell's way. Mother let her do whatever she wanted and now she does as she pleases, no matter the effect on our family or her reputation. Truthfully though, she's been shaping up the longer this goes on. She just can't help herself some days."

The three young men fell silent as Lord Harrington stood, waiting with baited breath for the promised birching.

"Please Father," her sweet young voice drifted up to their ears, pleading. "This is really quite unnecessary."

"It's not for you to decide what's necessary," said her father, gesturing impatiently for her to get up. "If you hadn't worn that dress then it would have been unnecessary. I'm burning it this afternoon and if you get any more like it then you'll be punished even more harshly. You deliberately disobeyed me, deceived your brother into

4

thinking you were properly attired and have brought shame down on our family. The number of people who saw you so immodestly displayed at such an early hour is not to be thought of. The Society matrons will pick you apart before we ever have a chance to present you and then you'll never be wed."

Eleanor's pretty blonde head was bowed, making her appear contrite, but the fists clenched at her sides told the real story. The anger in her body only intrigued Edwin more, he'd known she had some fire beneath her haughty exterior and now he was finally getting a chance to see some of it. His groin stirred as he peered down at her, remembering the lovely, creamy swell of her breast he'd been privileged to see this morning.

"From now on you'll present yourself to me before leaving the house so I can ensure you are never again so immodest in public. But for now, you will be punished for knowingly disobeying your father and causing further talk about town with your behavior. At this rate your reputation will be ruined before we ever reach London. Now get up and get into position."

Her movements jerky, Eleanor stood and walked around to the side of the chair, her back to the three hidden witnesses. Slowly she gripped her skirts and pull them up to her waist in back, extra fabric hanging down in the front. Edwin stifled a low moan at the sight of her buttoned boots, knee high stockings with garters, and thin white drawers; it was all he could do to keep from gasping as she leaned forward and it was revealed she was wearing the more old-fashioned kind of drawers, the kind lacking an inner seam. The fabric parted as she bent over the broad, padded arm of the chair, revealing creamy white buttocks and thighs, framed by the even whiter thin fabric of her undergarments.

"All the way in position, Eleanor," her father said sternly.

With a little whimper that hardened Edwin's cock even further, she spread her legs, pointing her toes inwards, which caused the blonde fringed shell of her cunny to spread, leaving it as bare and vulnerable as her arse.

Edwin's cock throbbed in his pants, fully at attention at this glorious sight and he surreptitiously put his hand over the bulge at the front of his pants, discreetly rubbing it as he watched his companions from the corner of his eye, but they were paying him no attention. Wesley's eyes were riveted to the scene below him and Hugh was watching as well, although with much less interest than Wesley or Edwin. Edwin refocused his attention there as Lord Harrington nodded his head approvingly and went to a side cupboard.

"He says that position's the best for a spanking or birching, it keeps her from clenching her buttocks," Hugh whispered in a lecturing tone, seeming to think it was his duty to provide his friends with the instruction his father had given him. That was something Edwin had known from school, although he didn't stop Hugh from talking. He was too entranced by the sight below; noticing the position also seemed to heighten Eleanor's vulnerability and humiliation. Indeed, her entire upper body, which was laid over the seat of the chair, seemed to declare her embarrassment to the young men, despite her ignorance that she had an audience. Her little white fists were clenched on either side of her head and Edwin thought he could see a pink flush on the back of her neck, as if she was so red in her face that the color had traveled across her pale skin to less usual locations.

The birch Lord Harrington pulled from the cupboard was tied with a red ribbon and was much lighter looking than the ones Edwin was familiar with from school, although it looked plenty long and whippy. He felt a small sense of relief that Eleanor wouldn't be subjected to the heavy rod young men were. After all, the pale glowing skin of her bottom looked much more delicate than any man's rump.

"There will be twenty strokes," Lord Harrington announced, ignoring his daughter's protest.

"That's more than he's ever given her before," Hugh whispered quickly. "The last time it was fifteen."

"If you move or try to cover yourself then we will start the counting over at one. I hope this helps you learn your lesson daughter; I'm very disappointed in you."

And with that, he laid the birch across her cheeks with a hard slap.

6

Eleanor's body tensed but she didn't make a sound, despite the red streaks now spreading across her creamy cheeks. Edwin rather felt like moaning himself. Although there was nothing inherently erotic about what Lord Harrington was doing, he found the sight of those creamy swells, marked with red, to be extremely arousing. Another hard slap, this one higher up on her rump and she jerked again. The third was applied firmly to her upper thighs, just beneath her cheeks, and the young men heard the first feminine wail as red streaks appeared on this more sensitive area. Two more strokes across her buttocks, laying over some of the stripes which had already been applied, and Eleanor's buttocks were turning a nice shade of pink even when red lines hadn't appeared.

The young woman was now gasping and crying, her legs obviously trembling with the effort of remaining in place, as her hips moved up and down, wagging her rump as she tried to escape the burning lash of the rod. Edwin had to grip his hands to keep from actually reaching inside of his pants to grip his cock, it was throbbing so hard inside of his breeches.

"Six," counted Lord Harrington as he landed another across the top of her rump, over the first one he had laid down. Eleanor shrieked.

"Please Papa, please, I've learned my lesson!" she begged, her voice full of tears.

"No, you haven't, for you are still trying to get out of your punishment," said her father, his voice weary, as if he despaired of his daughter ever learning her lesson. Three more hard lashes landed across her rump and Eleanor screamed, begging for her father to stop. Edwin was entranced by the sight of her bum, which was now a nice, bright cherry red, her cheeks clenching and dancing in between lashes. He rubbed his cock harder, feeling it throb underneath his hand, the fabric of his breeches moving over it. Out of the corner of his eye he saw Wesley doing the same, all of them were similarly affected by this sight of domestic discipline. Hugh seemed both oblivious and unaffected, watching with the critical eye of a student in a classroom. Of course, since it was his sister perhaps he couldn't see the appeal.

"Ten, eleven, twelve," intoned Lord Harrington as he peppered Eleanor's thighs, drawing new shrieks from her. Edwin knew from experience that thighs were more sensitive things than buttocks and he applied more pressure to his cock as he watched her legs start to come together, no longer under their mistress' control. Her father snapped two more lashes onto her inner thighs, forcing them back apart as Eleanor sobbed and begged.

"Please... no Papa... that's enough..."

"Fifteen," said Lord Harrington, landing another one. "And last time fifteen was not enough, so we will continue. Sixteen."

Eleanor's choked screams echoed around the room. Now her bottom was really moving, squirming and bouncing, as she buried her face into the seat of the chair and sobbed. Lord Harrington finished the last four strokes across her glowing red bottom.

As he returned the birch rod to its cupboard, the young men in the gallery were able to stare unimpeded at the sight of the sobbing and chastened Eleanor, her formerly creamy buttocks and thighs now hot and glowing, her cunny swollen and reddened. Edwin thought he might actually die from the intense state of arousal he was in; it might be wrong but at least Wesley had also been affected.

"Now go stand in the corner," Lord Harrington ordered as he turned around. "And keep your skirts up. I'll tell you when you can return to your room."

The Earl sat back down at his desk, returning to his ledgers as Eleanor minced her way to the corner, holding her skirts around her waist. Now the men were able to see her tear-streaked face and red eyes as she moved to do as her father directed.

Leaving the gallery quietly, Wesley asked Hugh why the corner.

"More embarrassing. He'll keep her there until at least one person comes into the room and sees her there."

"Do you think we could go?" asked Edwin, feeling desirous of seeing Eleanor's beaten buttocks closer.

Hugh thought about it and then shook his head. "He'll know I brought you there for the purpose of seeing her and I don't think he'd approve. It's one thing if one of the maids see her, another thing if it's a young man of her station."

Nodding his head in understanding, Edwin hastily made his excuses and left to go into town, feeling the insistent desire to find a willing woman and sink into her as soon as possible. Wesley left with him.

CHAPTER 1

*O*ne year later Edwin saw a very different Eleanor at her come-out ball than he had before the fateful day when he'd witnessed her birching, in fact rather different from the week he'd spent with her family in Brighton. She looked every inch the presentable young lady, demure and well-mannered, although Hugh said she occasionally still received a spanking for minor infractions. There seemed to be a spark in her pretty sapphire eyes though, as she surveyed the young men of the ballroom like a huntress searching for her prey. Edwin found himself intrigued, and not just because of the memory of her rosy, beaten buttocks, although that was part of it.

Since that time he'd found one or two ladies who were intrigued by having a spanking to their bare bottoms, and he'd found it had aroused him more than ever before. Once he'd caught one of his maids stealing from him and instead of turning her out he'd let her stay on after receiving a personal birching from him. The discipline had aroused both of them so much he'd broken one of his cardinal rules and taken her right then and there. Normally he never dallied with the staff, having learned his lesson from the first time he'd made one of the maids his mistresses, and the disruption it had caused in the household. Collette wasn't his mistress though, there had been that one time, but she had gone on to be married about a year later to a footman in a neighboring household. Edwin rather envied the lucky man. Still, neither Collette nor any of the other women had quite satisfied the need which had risen in him that first day when he'd witnessed Eleanor's birching. He sometimes wondered if it was because it was the first time he'd seen such a thing or if it had been Eleanor herself.

Lately, his own thoughts had turned to marriage. His parents were ensconced firmly in the countryside, but that didn't stop his mother from sending him constant letters inquiring as to the steps he was taking to find a wife. After all, he was her only child and if something were to happen to him then the title would go to a distant cousin. The last few letters his mother had sent had hinted at coming to London herself to offer her assistance. Considering how much either of his parents hated to leave the country, he didn't want her to feel as though it was necessary.

Now, tonight at this ball, he realized what he had been waiting for this past year. The milk and water misses held no allure for him, despite the fact that many of them were quite beautiful, they all bored him. He wanted a different kind of marriage. Not one where with he would have to respectfully knock on her door, request admittance, and then make boring, gentle love to, but a wife who had spirit, sensuality, passion, and preferably the occasional need to be disciplined. A wife like Collette's lucky husband had. Eleanor would make a splendid future Countess. Truthfully, she'd been hovering in the back of his mind constantly ever since he'd seen her birched. Of course, her late debut had caused a bit of gossip but he didn't care about that.

Although they'd only spent a week together during the previous year, and he had seen for himself what sharp-tongued brat Eleanor had turned into during that time, he also knew what she had been like before she turned spoiled. He knew she had once followed Hugh, Wesley, and himself around practically begging for attention, trailing her doll Rose along with her everywhere she went. He knew she'd worn pink for two years straight and refused to put on a dress in any other color. He remembered when she'd found some neighbor boys bullying one of the village girls and had chased them off before offering up her doll, Rose, for the little girl to play with. At that point he'd kept a sharp eye out in case one of the boys had wanted to retaliate against Eleanor, but they'd had the wits enough to realize it was best to leave the eight-year-old and her new six-year-old friend alone. There was still the sweet, generous spirit inside of her, he believed, it was just buried deep down under the desire for silks, jewels, and worshipful male attention.

Deciding he might as well get to know this new Eleanor so he could make an informed decision, Edwin crossed to her side of the room. Her debut dress was white, of course, and it looked quite well with her complexion, emphasizing the pink of her cheeks and lips, the bright gold of her hair and her shining blue eyes.

"Lady Harrington," he greeted her mother with a slight bow, smiling his most charming smile. "Lady Eleanor."

"Lord Hyde, you rogue," Lady Harrington said with a smile. "You've been staring at my Nell here for the past fifteen minutes and you're only just now coming to talk?" Edwin winked at her teasing, although he knew she also spoke the truth.

"I was too arrested by the sight of her beauty," he said smoothly, "and have only just now found my tongue again. You are looking particularly lovely tonight Lady Eleanor." The neckline of her gown was low but not immodest, in fact it was almost demure compared to some of the gowns other women in the room were wearing. He was quite sure he had seen Eleanor eying them enviously. Obviously still wanting things her father said she couldn't have.

"Since you have found your tongue again, one would think you would use it for something other than the usual banal compliments," Eleanor said a little waspishly. He hid a smile. Not because he wasn't offended at her brash remark, but because it was obvious she still had some of her spirit and a husband would have ample opportunity to discipline her if she couldn't get her waspish tongue under control.

"Eleanor!" said her mother in scandalized tones, fanning herself vigorously as if feeling faint. "You are being quite rude. Please do forgive her, my Lord." She fluttered her eyes at him. If this was an example of how Lady Harrington reproached her willful daughter, Edwin could well understand how Eleanor had become so spoiled under her care. Lady Harrington meant well, but she was not a disciplinarian the way her husband was.

The young lady's mouth puckered mulishly at her mother's apology, almost pouting in a way that made him want to bend his head down and kiss her, despite the ire in her eyes. "It's just Edwin, mother. We've known him forever." As if familiarity excused her rude behavior.

Smiling genially at Lady Harrington, Edwin turned a more rakish look on Eleanor. One which she hadn't seen on his face before, because he'd never turned his flirtatious charm on his friend's sister. Lowering his eyes, he leaned in closer and his smile broadened as she inhaled sharply, looking up at him in consternation.

IN TRUTH, Eleanor was quite intimidated by Lord Hyde, which is why she had sharpened her tongue on him, feeling as if she had something to prove. He was very tall, very muscular and very good looking, and having him in such close proximity to her, with her mother teasing him about staring at her, had pushed aside all the society masks she'd created since her father had taken a closer interest in her behavior. The number of spankings and birchings had subsided as she'd started bowing to her father's demands and wishes, no matter how much she chafed over his unfair rules. After all, look at the number of young debutantes here with much more bosom showing than herself, in finer fabrics and with better jewelry! This was her coming out ball and she should have shone; instead she was stuck in a dress that catered to her father's stupid and old-fashioned ideals.

Over the past year she'd learned to keep her thoughts to herself, to pretend to be acquiescent with her father's demands, and to show herself as the perfect little society miss. It was all part of her plan to remove herself from her father's strict household as soon as possible, once she was a wife she could do as she pleased, buy all the clothes and fripperies she wanted, and her husband would shower her with expensive jewelry. Eleanor knew exactly what she wanted in a husband—a man who loved her to distraction.

She'd seen the way her parents' marriage worked; her mother loved her father unconditionally and bowed to his every wish. They'd spent the last six years in Brighton and she'd never managed to forget the day when she'd overheard her mother asking her husband if he was sure he didn't want her and Eleanor to stay in London with him and he'd responded, "For God's sake, Penelope, go to Brighton! If you aren't there by next week I'll make sure you regret it!"

And they'd spent the last six years there, rarely going into London for more than a weekend and her father had rarely come to visit them for more than a few weeks. Although he did make the trip quite often, he spent the majority of his time in London with Hugh. Eleanor had felt more than a little neglected, not to mention outraged on the part of her mother who was always sad when her father was absent, and she'd vowed that such a thing would never happen to her.

Although she felt sure her father cared about her mother, he obviously didn't care enough and he didn't love her enough to keep her with him, no matter how much Lady Harrington missed him. Eleanor would not fall in love. The person who was *not* in love had the power and that's what Eleanor wanted, a comfortable life with a man who would worship her and lavish gifts upon her.

Already she'd flirted with several young men who would do quite nicely. Lord Kilcairn had practically tripped over himself to be the first to secure a dance with her, the second son of the Marquess of Salisbury had begged to fetch her a lemonade and the young Earl of Cawdor had promised to talk to his aunt, Lady Cowper, about securing her permission to waltz. There were plenty of other men in the room looking at her with admiring eyes whom she hadn't even been introduced to yet, although she knew she would be soon. Perhaps she'd even let a few of them take her out on the terrace and kiss her. After all, her debut had come after most of her friends' and so she had some catching up to do—all of *them* had been kissed at least once.

Lord Hyde was certainly not on her list of possible husbands. He was too large, too intimidating, too disturbing. The way he looked at her made her feel like he was undressing her with those unfathomable dark eyes; they were admiring of her but there was nothing puppy-like about it. Tonight he was looking particularly fine in a light grey coat that set off his dark hair and eyes and emphasized his shoulders, breeches molding themselves to his muscular legs, and a charcoal waistcoat that hugged his masculine figure. The slightly amused and yet somehow intense expression on his face did nothing to soothe her anxiety around him. The roguish smile he gave her only affirmed her wariness of him, but it also made her insides tighten in the most inexplicable way.

"I could never deny a request from you, Lady Harrington," he said, in his smooth, deep voice. Shivers ran up her spine and she could feel gooseflesh breaking out all over her body. She didn't remember him ever having quite this effect on her before. It was incredibly unnerving. Had he ever looked at her quite that way before? "However, I do believe that apologies are more appreciated coming from the source of the offense."

He looked at her expectantly.

A sharp retort was on the tip of her tongue when she saw her father approaching out of the corner of her eye. Immediately she bowed her head, knowing her mother wouldn't say anything to her father about her misbehavior if only she could apologize and change the topic before he came within earshot.

"Please forgive me, my lord," she said in a mild, soft tone, giving a small curtsy. "I'm afraid I am overly excited by the importance of this evening and temporarily lost my manners."

"Of course," said Lord Hyde. She peeked up at him through her lashes, wondering at the tone in his voice. Was he amused by her? Fury pinked her cheeks, but she couldn't say anything because her father had just reached their group. He exchanged greetings with Lord Hyde and asked if Edwin would call on him the next day. Having agreed to do so, Lord Hyde then turned and asked Eleanor for a dance.

With her father watching she couldn't do anything but say yes, as graciously as possible. Once on the dance floor she kept on her smooth social mask, finding it the only defense she had against Lord Hyde's heated eyes and probing glances.

"So how does it feel to be the most beautiful woman in the room?" he murmured as they passed each other, his hand lingering in hers just a moment too long.

"Don't allow Miss Cuthbert to hear you say that to me or her heart will be quite broken," she retorted, having seen the way the pretty debutante had sighed before, during, and after her dance with Edwin. But he only laughed. Obviously careless of what hearts he might be breaking and so Eleanor hardened hers, knowing he was a teasing rake. The kind of man her mother had warned her about, and the kind of man she already knew she wanted to avoid, not just because of his reputation, but because she knew he would never be malleable in the way she wished her future husband to be.

Yet that didn't stop her heart from pounding when he leaned over and whispered in her ear. "Miss Cuthbert is quite beautiful, but a man always has his preferences."

And his eyes dipped down to observe the creamy swells of her breasts. Beneath the fabric of her dress she could feel her nipples pucker and she found herself suddenly breathless. His words were not inappropriate, but his meaning was quite clear and made her glad, for the first time that evening, of her gown's modest neckline.

All in all, other than the dance with Lord Hyde, Eleanor's come-out was deemed a success by both her and her parents (although, of course, both of her parents counted that dance as part of her success). Her mother was happy because everything had gone smoothly, her father was happy because Eleanor had behaved—her mother neglected to inform him of his daughter's rude words to Lord Hyde and the walk on the terrace she'd taken with the Earl of Cawdor —and Eleanor was happy because she'd begun her campaign on two eligible young gentleman who seemed suitably malleable and easily infatuated. She was quite sure that removing herself from her parent's house and into a pampered marriage, where she could return to the lifestyle she'd formerly led before her father took such an interest in her upbringing, would commence by the end of the Season.

Putting on her most flirtatious smile, she turned her efforts for the night into finding her a malleable husband as soon as possible.

AT TEN O'CLOCK SHARP, Edwin presented himself at Lord Harrington's house. Most of the household was still abed, including Hugh, but Lord Harrington was already up and working in his study, which is where he received Edwin. Ten o'clock was rather early for Edwin when he was in town, but he hadn't wanted to deny Lord Harrington's request. His friend's father had seem rather serious when he'd made it and Edwin wanted to put his best foot forward, since he'd decided last night that Eleanor was eminently suitable to be his wife.

Indeed, he'd gone to bed with visions of her red, dancing bottom in his head. While she put on a remarkable show of being a meek, presentable miss, it was obvious she still had most of her rough edges and spoiled manners; catching her in those moments would be a delight. The idea of rousing her passions had made him as desirous of her as his craving to have her over his knee. The flare of attraction between them had been impossible to ignore and he'd seen the way she'd responded, despite the sharpness of her tongue.

Yet, he'd also been relieved to see evidence she was the same sweet girl he'd once known. Because he'd kept a close watch on her the entire ball he hadn't failed to miss when she'd gone amongst the wall-flowers, taking her trailing train of gentlemen with her and skillfully setting them to dance with the other young ladies. Some of whom hadn't danced all evening prior to Eleanor's efforts. More so, she'd done it in such a way that the young ladies blossomed under Eleanor's smiling gaze, drawing them into conversations with the young men. Although he'd also noticed there had been two or three gentlemen she hadn't relinquished from her side, and he'd taken careful note of them, especially the overeager Kilcairn whom she seemed to save her most engaging smiles for. Young puppy.

"Thank you for coming so early, Lord Hyde," Lord Harrington said as he set his work aside. Edwin sat at attention. He'd always respected Lord Harrington and looked to him as a model for behavior, even before he'd known about his methods of discipline. Now he studied the man opposite him, a fine looking gentleman with silvering blonde hair, laugh lines about his mouth and at the corners of his light blue eyes. However, his hair was so light colored already, one could barely tell he was going silver, so he ended up looking much younger than his years. "I know town hours usually dictate a later start in the day for most young men of your age and I appreciate your promptness."

"Of course, my Lord," Edwin said.

"Edwin," Lord Harrington dropped the formality now they were past their greetings, "it has come to my attention you are a fine, upstanding young gentleman, and you seem to have moved past the wild ways of many young men rather early in life. I commend you for your maturity, and it is that maturity which has led me to consider putting a proposal forward to you."

Curious now, Edwin leaned forward a little. Lord Harrington seemed almost nervous, his forearms folded in front of him on the desk, a rather anxious expression on his face. "I'm flattered you hold me in such high esteem, my Lord, as I have always held you. I am happy to hear any proposal you have for me, please continue."

"As Hugh may have told you, preparing Eleanor for presentation to Society has not been... the easiest task. I noticed your interest in my daughter last night and I also know from Hugh that you run a disciplined household, and you know and approve of my methods for curbing the worst of Eleanor's excesses. She needs a firm hand and traditional methods. Despite the progress I have made with her in the past few years I am convinced she means to marry some wilting dandy who will let her have her head and she will end up shaming us all. That's if she doesn't ruin herself first, which seems all too likely based on her behavior last night." Lord Harrington winced, as if remembering something particularly bad, and Edwin wondered what on earth Eleanor had done last night. He had left by the time Eleanor had taken her walk on the terrace with Lord

Cawdor, a walk she hadn't hidden as well from her father as she'd thought. "If you are amenable, I would like you to consider taking Eleanor as your wife."

Edwin's heart pounded in his chest with excitement. How strange and unusual that Lord Harrington should offer him the very thing he'd been hoping to one day present to the Lord. Still, perhaps it wouldn't do to seem over eager. This was an unusual request from a debutante's father so early in the Season after all, were there circumstances he was unaware of?

"My Lord, I am honored you thought of me, but this is very sudden is it not? Is Eleanor ah..." he paused, unsure of how to delicately phrase the question. Not that he truly cared if she was ruined, as long as there were no consequences which would have repercussions for his family, but he would like to know what he was getting into.

"She's not ruined," Lord Harrington said bluntly, and Edwin coughed to hide his embarrassment at being so transparent. "No, I'm not angry, I can understand your concern. The problem is I'm worried she'll attract some young buck who won't be able to handle her and convince him to elope to Gretna Green with her. I'd like to get her married off to a *suitable* man before that happens. Despite her progress in manners, none of the young men she surrounded herself with last night are what I would consider suitable and if I don't intervene now she'll either convince one of them to marry her or someone *will* ruin her. I don't want her to be unhappy. You're a young and attractive man, you've known her and the family since you were a boy and I know I can trust you to take care of her. The only other men who might be able to handle her are much older and I think she would object to that. There seemed to be something between the two of you last night when you spoke and then danced. I think once she realizes she has a husband who won't take any of her nonsense, she'll prove herself to be an asset as your lady wife and you two will be as happy as your parents or my wife and I."

Now leaning forward, Lord Harrington's body language communicated his earnestness clearly. He truly was concerned about his daughter, as well as his family's name, and he wanted to be able to trust Edwin to take care of her. But he also needed Edwin to keep her from disgracing herself, if they were to marry.

"I would certainly like to make her happy," said Edwin truthfully, although his ideas on how to do so were much more closely aligned with her father's than with the lady's own. "However, I'm not quite sure you've made as much progress as you think." He described Eleanor's rude behavior from the night before as Lord Harrington's face darkened, ending with a request she not be punished as he'd rather not have her feeling any more antagonistic towards him than necessary at this juncture.

"Thank you for telling me," Lord Harrington said. "I will allow you to handle it as you see fit. Please rest assured her mother will be suitably chastened for not informing me of our daughter's antics." Edwin shot him a look of surprise and Lord Harrington smiled. "Ah, you thought the Lady is exempt from the discipline of the house? Absolutely not. In fact, you will find that disciplining a wife is altogether a different thing from disciplining a daughter."

"I see, my Lord," said Edwin feeling rather stunned. The idea of the demure and graceful Lady Harrington bent over the arm chair—which happened to be the one he was sitting in—to receive a spanking from her husband was both shocking and rather arousing itself as he realized how many delightful years he would have ahead of him with Eleanor. "Well, I should be very happy to marry Eleanor. Last night I had the thought that she would make an ideal wife for me, although I had planned on courting her properly."

Lord Harrington waved his hand dismissively. "No time for that, she'd just use it to get into more trouble. The sooner I shackle you two together, the happier I'll be."

They hammered out the marriage agreement rather quickly after the solicitors were called to join them, with Lord Harrington looking extremely relieved now that he knew his daughter would be in good hands, assured she would have no chance to dishonor or shame their family with a stalwart and responsible husband like Lord Hyde. Promising to return that afternoon to propose, Edwin left to secure a special license so he and Eleanor could marry on the morrow.

CHAPTER 2

"What?!" Eleanor asked her father, staring at him completely aghast. Her hands clenched in the skirt of her father-approved modest beige morning gown; she felt faint for the first time in her life. This could not be happening.

"You will marry Lord Hyde tomorrow," her father said calmly, before continuing to new information as if he hadn't just announced the most awful fate imaginable. "It's quite a good match, I believe." He was smiling, so obviously proud of himself for arranging her marriage that she wanted to scream.

"But it's too soon! My debut was *yesterday!*" she protested, her mind racing. The fact that he had made her insides quiver last night didn't make a basis for a good marriage, and Lord Hyde's strong personality certainly didn't make for the kind of marriage Eleanor wanted. Somehow she instinctively knew he wouldn't be at all malleable or inclined to give her whatever she wanted. After all, heated glances and seductive words or not, he'd known her for too long, had heard her waspish tongue. There would be no honeying her way with sweet words and promises when it came to him. After all her hard work attracting an acceptable court of suitors, and her father was going to cut her off from them before she could even attempt to bring one up to snuff!

"You're lucky I let you come out at all with the way you ended up behaving," her father said sternly, his smile fading a little. "I certainly hope you aren't arguing with me Eleanor. This is a good match. He's young, wealthy, and eager to wed you. You could do much worse."

She could also do much better. Eleanor shook her head, furious, unable to verbalize her thoughts, and her father's smile faded further, his face darkening.

"Eleanor, you will marry him. Tomorrow. He will be here to propose this afternoon and you will accept him."

"Please Papa, don't make me do this," she begged, reduced to it by her panic. "I don't want to marry him."

The look on his face darkened even more and solidified. "You want to marry one of those idiots you can push around, is that it? Lord Cawdor or Count Bryant? Yes, I saw you leading them around last night. They're not worthy of a woman like you, and the fact you would even consider lowering yourself to marrying one of those buffoons only highlights the need for someone wiser to make such important decisions for you. Count Bryant is heavily in debt thanks to his gaming habits and Lord Cawdor doesn't have the wit or the will to keep you in line, you'd ruin both his good name and ours within a month."

That was exactly why she was interested in Cawdor. Bryant hadn't been one of the men she favored, but Cawdor would have done perfectly. Although, of course, she wouldn't have ruined him, but she would have had all the beautiful dresses she wanted, and dripping jewels, a husband who would adore her and… everything. She shook her head again, wanting so badly to stamp her foot and scream and throw the kind of tantrum she used to indulge in up to a few years ago. "I won't!"

Lord Harrington sighed, somehow instinctively knowing it would come to this. His wife had indulged their daughter far too long and he hadn't been paying proper attention or he would have put a stop to it much sooner. Now it was too late and he could only be thankful that Edwin, who was already wise to some of Eleanor's tricks and wouldn't allow her to run wild, had been so interested in her. As much as he would have liked to give Eleanor a proper debut, she'd already shown last night that she couldn't be trusted to be a proper lady.

"You will. Last night you came within a hairsbreadth of shaming the family. Do you know how many matrons saw you leave for a walk about the terrace with Lord Cawdor? And come in looking flushed, like you'd just been kissed?" Eleanor winced, because of course the truth was she *had* just enjoyed her first kiss. "You were almost ruined at your *come-out* ball Eleanor. I will not give you the opportunity to actually do so. If you continue to argue I will spank you."

"But Papa, surely you can't—"

Her father stood, patience wrung out that she was still trying to fight with him. "Over the chair Eleanor."

"No, Papa, please!" Immediately her voice turned pleading, cajoling, the way it always did when she knew she'd gone too far. And, as always, it didn't work at all.

"You're trying my patience Eleanor. You are my daughter and your duty is to obey. I have indulged this conversation long enough. Position yourself over the chair."

Letting out a small sob, Eleanor indulged in stamping her feet as she got into position. It did very little to vent her emotions; she should have left when he told her to and now she bitterly regretted not doing so. By now she'd learned her father didn't bluff. Lifting up her skirts was the worst part, baring her bottom and vulnerable places for punishment. None of her other friends ever mentioned having to do anything remotely like this, not since they were small children, only her father was so old fashioned and stodgy. They got to wear prettier dresses than her too, with lower necklines, in better fabrics, and go shopping whenever they wanted. They didn't receive lectures about proper behavior or immodest gowns. It didn't occur to Eleanor that most of her friends who were currently unmarried didn't actually need those lectures, as they were more firmly under the control of their mothers', whom were all much stricter than her own.

She could hear him opening the cupboard and she winced. *Please not the birch*, she thought. Unfortunately she was not much heartened to hear the familiar slap of the leather tawse against her father's open palm.

"Ten strokes and I hope this is the last time I will have to punish you," he said. "After all, you marry tomorrow and then you are his responsibility."

The last time? Suddenly Eleanor didn't feel quite so bad. Surely things would be different in Lord Hyde's house. And perhaps she could contrive some manner to escape; if she put off being bedded for long enough then she could run away and have the marriage annulled later, couldn't she?

Leather whistled through the air and landed with a crack across the round globes of her bottom.

"One."

Gritting her teeth, Eleanor dug her hands into the leather cushion on the seat of the chair. The last time. She could get through this. Another stroke landed, just below the first, and air hissed out between her teeth.

"Three," she heard her father say as pain flared through her thighs.

Burying her head in the chair, she let herself cry her way through her last punishment, her heated buttocks twitching as the strap fell on it again and again. She would find a way out of this. She might not be able to avoid marrying Edwin, but once out of her father's household she would find a way to have the marriage annulled and then she could have the life she wanted, the life she had planned for. She would be loved and adored, not dictated to and disciplined or sent away to Brighton to languish.

"Ten."

The last stroke fell and Eleanor let out a long sigh of relief. Although her buttocks felt fiery and sore, they didn't hurt nearly as bad as some of the punishments she'd received in the past. And this was her last one.

"Now what do you say, Eleanor?"

"I'm sorry Father, for disobeying and arguing with you. I know you only want what is best for me." The truth of those words suddenly struck her. Although she might hate her father's methods, she didn't doubt his love or that he wanted her to have a secure and happy life, they just disagreed on what would make that life for her.

Something of her thoughts must have shown in her face because her father smiled at her, perhaps hearing the ring of sincerity in her voice.

"I do Eleanor, I really do." To her surprise, he embraced her gently and didn't tell her to stand in the corner before giving her permission to leave the room. "Oh, and Eleanor? Could you tell your mother I'd like to see her in here?"

WHEN EDWIN WAS SHOWN into the salon that afternoon Eleanor and her mother were both sitting on the sofa looking rather uncomfortable. The redness around both of their eyes indicated that tears had been shed sometime in the past few hours and they were shifting uncomfortably, as if their bottoms hurt. Had Lord Harrington already administered a punishment to his wife? Had he gone back on his word about disciplining Eleanor or had she earned a red bottom for something else?

Wondering if his future wife had been soundly spanked this afternoon made Edwin's breeches feel rather tight, but he tried to push such enticing thoughts out of his head for a more appropriate time. After exchanging the usual courtesies and a few comments about the weather, Lady Harrington excused herself, claiming a need to find her maid, ostensibly to give Edwin and Eleanor a few minutes alone so he might propose.

For herself, Eleanor was so wrapped up in herself she hadn't even noticed her mother's discomfort or red eyes, even when she and her mother had been having a discussion about Lord Hyde's attributes and her mother's joy over her daughter's 'happy match.' It was all enough to make Eleanor want to slap Lord Hyde across his smug, handsome face. Yet nothing stopped the tremor through her body as he moved to seat himself next to her on the couch, far too close to her for comfort.

Oh, what was her father thinking? The hastiness of this match would cause more gossip than anything Eleanor had done. Although, since she and Edwin had known each other for so long, perhaps the gossip wouldn't be quite as bad, it wasn't as if they were strangers after all. He was one of her brother's closest friends. Looking into his dark, brooding eyes, she couldn't stop the flush that came to her cheeks. Unconsciously she shifted away from him, wincing as the weight on her sore bottom changed.

"Lady Eleanor," Edwin murmured, bringing her gaze back up to meet his. Her crystal blue eyes were filled with anxiety and excitement, the little catch in her breath as he leaned closer to her telling him she was not unaffected by his presence.

"Lord Hyde," she said, her voice formal, stilted. Yet the look she was giving him was of an innocent, awaiting a stolen kiss, with her head and lips tilted just so. It was an instinctive response and not one she would have made knowingly.

Sliding down onto one knee in front of her, Edwin impertinently put his hand on her thigh. Eleanor drew in her breath quickly as his hand seemed to sear her skin through the fabric of her gown. No man had ever touched her in such an inappropriate spot before. If only he wasn't so handsome, so big—so exciting… her reaction to his touch was more than a little disturbing to her.

"Eleanor," he said, his voice becoming more warmly intimate as he used her Christian name. Her cheeks flushed becomingly. "We've known each other for years now and last night at your ball I realized I'd never seen another woman I wanted to make my wife, not until I really looked at you and saw the young woman you've become and not the little girl I'd known all my life." His hand reached up and brushed her cheek. Eleanor jerked back. The touch of skin on skin was too fiery to be borne, although it didn't help when his hand settled back onto her thigh. The ring of truth in his voice disconcerted her, he actually sounded as if he was saying nothing but the honest truth. Was it possible he truly had a hidden *tendre* for her?

That he truly wanted to marry her for something other than her father's money or request? The idea appealed more than she wanted to admit. "I know this is quite sudden, but I want you to understand this is what I truly want. Please, do me the honor of becoming my wife."

There was no mention of love or adoration in his little speech, but she didn't doubt his words. Edwin had never been a liar and there was sincerity in everything he said, although she couldn't account for why he was suddenly speaking of these feelings now. Perhaps he would be easier to influence than she thought. Surprisingly flustered, Eleanor cleared her throat to try and find her voice, it came out in a husky whisper.

"I had no idea..." she cleared her throat again. While she still wasn't sure marriage to Lord Hyde was what she wanted, at the very least it would get her out of her father's house. Then she could find a way to annul the marriage and flee to her mother in Brighton, surely one of her swains would be willing to meet her there and elope to Gretna Green. Kilcairn or Cawdor would probably consider it the height of heroic romance. That was probably for the best, her strange attraction to Edwin was dangerous and not to be indulged. But for now she must play the part she had been assigned. "I accept."

He gave her a wry grin, as if acknowledging her rather lackluster response. Then, to her shock, he stood, pulling her to her feet and into his arms in one swift movement.

"What are you—?" she started to say before he cut her off.

"Let us seal it with a kiss."

Then his lips were on hers. They were soft, warm, and insistent. Eleanor shuddered at the sensation of his strong arms wrapped around her, easily holding her against him. The muscles of his broad chest flexed under her hands as she pushed at him. Then one of his hands slid down her back and squeezed her bottom, eliciting a small gasp of pain as his fingers dug into her abused rear. Edwin took advantage of her open lips to slide his tongue into her mouth. He tasted of spice and mint, his tongue both shocking and exciting her, as did this entire encounter. Somehow the heat in her bottom seemed to change under Edwin's hand, from a renewed sting to something arousing. Making a small mewling noise Eleanor squirmed against him, although she was no longer entirely sure she wanted him to let her go. Something new and fantastic had flared to life inside of her, making her sore bottom feel almost good as his hand squeezed it, and she could feel herself yearning for… something…

With a show of willpower Edwin considered nothing less than heroic, he released Eleanor's soft, curvy body, reluctantly letting go of her luscious bottom. While it was possible she had gasped because she was shocked at the liberties he'd taken by touching her so intimately, Edwin was sure he'd heard some pain in her voice, meaning she certainly had at least been spanked before he came over. The idea inflamed him. Spanked the day before being wedded to him and soon he'd have the right to put his hands all over her lovely body. To administer that discipline.

For her part, Eleanor stared at him, very much like an awed child as her body trembled now that he was no longer holding her up. What on earth had just happened? Why had she responded to him like that?

The man was more dangerous than she'd realized. While she'd heard about the effect a rake could have on an innocent young woman, she had never experienced it for herself and had no idea it was so overwhelming. A man like this wouldn't be controlled by her. There was no way she could marry him.

"Ah, is everything alright in here?" her mother said, appearing in the doorway to see them standing and staring at each other.

"Quite," said Lord Edwin with a smile as he turned to face her, taking Eleanor's hand in his. "I have asked the Lady Eleanor to be my wife and she has accepted my proposal."

"Oh how wonderful!" exclaimed Lady Harrington, as if the news was unexpected. "I am thrilled to be the first to wish you happy."

Eleanor gave her mother a sickly smile, the best she could do under the circumstances. Oh… how was she going to get out of this?

MARRIED. The slim gold band around her finger seemed more like a shackle, chaining her to the charming, handsome man at her side who was smiling as if he'd just won a fortune at White's. Somehow, despite the short notice, her parents had managed to round up a small assembly of guests, including one young lady she suspected was included for her brother's benefit. Miss Irene Chandler was the daughter of Baron Standish. It was well known that Miss Chandler's family wasn't very flush and her dowry didn't have any money, but was a bit of land which abutted directly next to some of Lord Harrington's. If Hugh and Miss Chandler were to marry then, the land would become part of the Harrington estate, something Eleanor knew her father wanted.

Miss Chandler was quite beautiful, with strawberry-blonde hair and shining emerald eyes. In her third Season she had a number of suitors, but none so far who were quite willing to propose marriage, knowing that doing so would mean taking on the financial burdens of her family. It was a well-known fact she would need a wealthy husband and none of her suitors came close to the wealth or status Hugh did. Despite it being an arranged marriage, Hugh showed every sign of being a bit smitten with the young lady, dancing his attendance on her all through Eleanor and Edwin's wedding breakfast. He'd always had a much more romantic nature than his sister.

The wedding breakfast was coming to a close and soon Eleanor would be off to her new husband's town home. Anxiety roiled in her stomach. So many changes!

"Eleanor are you alright?" The concern in her father's voice sparked tears in her eyes.

"Yes Father... I just...." She paused, not wanting to insult her new husband. Not in front of him at least. "Everything's changing."

"Ah," her father said smiling before turning to her new husband. "Edwin, might I have a moment with my daughter?"

"Of course, sir," Edwin said, giving her hand a squeeze before he walked across the room to speak to Hugh, pausing a few times to receive the well wishes of the other guests. Eleanor watched him, her heart in her throat. Every little touch he gave her seemed to have that effect on her but she knew she must keep him out of her bed. Otherwise she wouldn't be able to annul the marriage.

Her father put his hand on her upper arm, drawing her attention back to him. The expression on his face was gentle.

"We'll miss having you in the house, Nell, but we'll be close by. I chose a good man for you. He'll provide the kind of environment you need."

"Yes Papa," she said, a lump forming in her throat. "I'll miss you too."

"Just be a good, obedient wife to him," her father said, grinning broadly. "He'll take good care of you. "

"I'll try, Papa," she said, mentally forgiving herself the lie. She would be good and obedient as much as she could for as long as she could, but she didn't consider this a real marriage anyway. Why, they hadn't even had a real wedding—she wasn't wearing a special dress, she didn't have a special bouquet, and there hadn't been rows and rows of guests filling a church to see her in all her splendor. And despite the elegance of this wedding breakfast, it was far too small. This barely counted as a wedding at all.

"See that you do."

On the other side of the room, her brother, Hugh, and Edwin were having their own conversation about Miss Chandler.

"Quite the beauty," Edwin said, although truthfully he preferred Eleanor's fair looks and lush hair. Miss Chandler was certainly beautiful however; quite slim with a porcelain complexion, pleasing features and young, high breasts, small but perfectly formed. Her hair was a light reddish color and she had stunning emerald eyes. Looking the perfect little queen, she sat and chatted with Lady Harrington, showing her manners were as good as anyone else's despite her father's lower status and her family's financial situation.

"Isn't she?" Hugh said, looking rather starry eyed as he glanced over at the lady in question. "I wasn't sure I wanted to fall in line when my father told me about her, but if we can get that bit of land then we'll be able to expand the wool manufacturing, and as soon as I saw her I lost any objections. She's sweet, demure, quiet... everything Nell isn't."

They both chuckled.

"I think she'll be the perfect wife," Hugh said with a definitive nod.

"Does she hold you in affection?"

"She seems to," said Hugh, although there was a bit of doubt in his voice. He shrugged. "At least, she seems to have no objections to the marriage and she certainly appreciates my attentions. There's no reason we won't fall in love, I'm certainly more than halfway there." He grinned suddenly. "I always did want a marriage like my parents'."

"When will you propose?" Edwin asked.

"Probably soon," Hugh said amiably. "I'd rather get this wedding business over with as soon as possible. Mother wasn't pleased that Father insisted on such a quick, quiet wedding for Eleanor. Means she'll probably go overboard to make up for it planning mine."

"Do you think Wesley might be home in time?"

"I hope so, although he'll still be in mourning." They looked at each other, the thought of the third member of their trio dimming their happiness slightly. Wesley's adventurous feet had taken him to India soon after they'd watched Eleanor's birching. Unfortunately, six months ago his father had been killed in a carriage accident and Wesley had been called home to do his duties. No one was quite sure when he would finally arrive, but they knew he was on his way. It had taken awhile to locate him with the news and then he'd had to wrap up whatever he was doing in India—some kind of business venture although that wasn't common knowledge. Gentlemen weren't supposed to sully their hands with business, but Wesley had been making a fortune and most of the *ton* wouldn't care too much where the money came from as long as he had it.

"Well, at least wait until Eleanor and I return home from our honeymoon."

Hugh chuckled. "You think I'd allow you to miss it? Besides, my mother will want at least three months to get everything together, there's no chance of it going off before you come home."

Nodding, Edwin's gaze returned to his bride. Eleanor was looking quite lovely in a silver and gold wedding dress which was quite modest. It wasn't quite the wedding he'd pictured either, but the important thing was that he was married to the only women he'd ever thought about marrying. He wondered if she still wore the old fashioned kind of drawers with no seam, making for easy access to a woman's body. The thought stirred him in a way he needed to avoid while still in company.

"Alright chap, I think it's time for me to focus my attentions on my bride."

"Careful there, that's my sister," Hugh said.

"I'll take care of her."

"I know. Just don't let her get too out of hand. It's easier to curb her behavior right away, if you let her get away with even a little thing, she'll run with it." Hugh sighed and then sent a wistful and approving glance at Miss Chandler. Chuckling, Edwin shook his head. He'd much rather have a spirited and passionate bride than the quiet dutiful type, but he supposed after living with Eleanor, Miss Chandler must seem rather restful to Hugh.

The men shook hands and Edwin returned to his bride so they could take their leave of the company and return to his house. His parents rode in the carriage with them, making light conversation before dropping them at his town home where Edwin promptly introduced her to the household staff before she pleaded her tiredness and was allowed to retreat upstairs to her chamber for a refreshing nap.

DINNER WAS an uncomfortable affair for Eleanor. Her husband's hungry gaze made her quite nervous, despite the fact she was wearing one of the demure gowns her father approved of. She was quite sure she could feel Edwin's eyes lingering on the swell of her bosom. And he spent most of dinner explaining what he expected from her in terms of running the household. There was quite a bit of it and while Eleanor knew her mother took care of many of the small details of their household, it wasn't something she'd ever had to personally do and she knew very well Edwin had a housekeeper who had been taking care of it before he had a bride. Why could that not continue? But she didn't want to argue with him. At least not yet; she was quite sure the argument would come later when he wanted to bed her.

To begin her excuses, as soon as dinner was over she pleaded exhaustion and said she needed more rest. Fortunately, Edwin didn't seem at all suspicious, he even offered to walk her to her chambers. Relieved at his agreeableness, Eleanor smiled and accepted. She was rather torn between the suspicion that Edwin was much more dictatorial than he was currently showing and this new charming affability of her husband. Perhaps this wasn't such a bad arrangement after all, but she'd rather wait a few days and see. After all, Edwin had been chosen by her father and she'd wanted to be married in order to get away from her father's strictures.

Walking to her room they chatted amiably and Eleanor found herself wondering if she was bucking the idea of marriage to him because she was so used to wanting to defy her father. So far, Edwin didn't seem a bad sort of husband at all.

Pushing open the door to her room she turned to wish him a good night, and then he was on her, just as when he'd proposed. Eleanor found herself stumbling back into her room, Edwin's strong arms supporting her body and the door closing behind them. His lips were demanding, seductive, and she opened her mouth without thinking to accept his tongue. While her body reacted to his touch, his heat, her mind hastened to catch up. But it was so hard to think! He was so large and overwhelming, his hands hot on her neck as he pulled pins from her hair.

When he pulled his mouth from hers she was left gasping, her lips swollen from his kisses, as he began to lick and nibble his way down her sensitive neck. Dear God! The small, heated touches made the insides of her body tighten.

She'd always dismissed the romantic novels other young women read as silly twiddle twaddle, all those women who became wrapped up in a man's arms and immediately forgot everything was obviously an exaggeration. Now she was discovering she had been ignorant and overconfident. Her inexperienced body had never felt sensations like these before, she had no defenses to handle the hot wash of need surging through her. The area between her legs ached unbearably and when Edwin put his hands on her rear and pulled that part of her into his body, his thigh thrusting between her legs so she rubbed up against him, she realized he held the key to the hunger growing inside of her.

"Edwin... please..." she said, not entirely sure what she was asking for. She knew she needed to stop him, yet she couldn't formulate the words through her gasping breaths as he rocked his leg between hers.

"Lovely, lovely Eleanor," he said into her ear, nibbling on the lobe in a way that made her want to melt. "So clever, claiming tiredness after you had such a long nap. If I'd known you were so eager I would have joined you earlier."

Dimly it occurred to Eleanor that her new husband had mistaken her intentions, but before she could tell him so, his hand slipped into the top of her gown and palmed her breast, tweaking her nipple between his fingers. Pleasure surged and she found herself going weak in the knees. Somehow, she wasn't entirely sure how, Edwin got her undressed much faster than any maid she'd ever had, seducing and bewildering her senses with caresses and nibbles as he did so.

Eleanor found herself on her back on the bed, completely bared to her husband's gaze, as he knelt over her dressed in just a shirt and breeches. Before she could protest, his hard body lowered onto hers and he kissed her deeply, his hands caressing her sensitive skin. Warmth blossomed everywhere his fingers touched her and she groaned into his mouth as he conquered her body.

"So soft," he murmured, moving down as he kissed her neck again, then moved down to her breasts.

"Edwin... I wasn't... oh goodness..." Eleanor's eyelids fluttered as he sucked one rosy nipple into his mouth, his hands cupping her breasts. Pinching her free nipple between two fingers, he rolled it back and forth, his mouth busy nibbling and suckling the other roseate nub. It was exquisite ecstasy and she bucked beneath him, feeling the weight of his hard body between her legs. Logic and sanity was quickly sinking into a vast sea of sensation and pleasure, the needy ache between her legs only growing more insistent as Edwin did the most sinful things to her nipples. She'd had no idea a man's touch could make her feel like this.

For his part, Edwin was more than pleased at his bride's passionate core. She was more than beautiful and he'd held her in affection even before he'd thought of spanking her himself. Now knowing what a passionate creature she was he was even more intrigued by her. The creaminess of her skin was quite pleasing and she had very pale and sensitive nipples. He enjoyed the small noises she made in the back of her throat as he toyed with them.

Kissing his way down her soft stomach, he was pleased to smell her arousal. Pushing her thighs apart he ignored her protest and stared at her dewy center with its thatch of pale blonde curls. It smelled divine, the delicate pink petals innocently tempting, and the little bud of her clitoris peeking at him from under its hood quite shyly. With a small groan of desire Edwin fell upon her.

Eleanor gasped and reached down to push him away as her husband put his mouth on her in the most shameful manner. "No... you can't... oooh..."

Unfortunately, that was the moment when she realized she must be a complete wanton, because rather than pushing him away she ended up gripping his dark hair and moaning as he did the most sinful things with his tongue. Something so depraved shouldn't feel so... fantastic. The small moans he made into her sensitive flesh as he made his way to her core with his lips vibrated through her and she found herself gripping his head with not just her hands, but also with her thighs.

All the tension coiling inside her was now cresting and Eleanor felt as though she was losing her grip on reality.

The sighs and moans she was making only urged Edwin onward. He'd always enjoyed pleasuring a lady with his mouth but he'd never had one react quite so dramatically. Then again, he'd never been with a virgin or a woman who was completely ignorant of sensual pleasure.

Smugly he congratulated himself on his choice of wife. Not only was she delicious in every sense of the word, her innocent reluctance and reactions were more arousing than any other woman he'd ever encountered. Perhaps that was partly because she truly was innocent with no prior experience on what could be done to her tender flesh or how to resist the sensation running through her body. More experienced women could handle their reactions better, control their desires. Eleanor had no such defense. Knowing he was the first man to touch her in this way inflamed him. Other women would have other men, but Eleanor was all his.

She cried out his name again, her sweet honey flowing copiously as he lapped it up. Her pink pearl was now fully engorged, no longer hiding beneath its hood, but swollen and blushing as he sucked it into his mouth, increasing her cries. Pressing a finger into her exquisite body, he nearly groaned at the tightness of her feminine tunnel.

Eleanor was shocked at the rude finger probing her most intimate space, yet there was nothing she could do to stop her husband. Already he'd put his mouth on her and elicited the most incredible sensations from her resistant body. Now her muscles felt like jelly and yet he was starting the sinful cycle all over again!

The tongue on her flesh never ceased, although now it was taking long sure strokes around the invading digit between her petals. Looking down the length of her pale body, she could see her nipples were still slightly budded, her skin flushed with exertion, and her husband's head bobbing between her thighs. His dark eyes looked up at her, meeting her gaze with such a heated look that she blushed even deeper, if that was possible. Eleanor covered her eyes, unable to bear looking at the perverse vision of her husband's depravities on her body, and just gave herself over to enjoying it.

Another finger pushed alongside the first, stretching her virgin tunnel further and Eleanor squirmed, squeezing her eyes shut. Somehow it made the experience less real, less invasively intimate, although it also meant she was more focused on the sensations her husband was causing in her body. Fingers moved back and forth, curving inside of her and brushing against a spot that made everything tighten convulsively. Edwin nibbled at her sensitive flesh and Eleanor gasped and writhed for him, mewling with the pleasure rising inside of her again.

"Oh Edwin..." she moaned, clutching at the bed sheets beneath her. The wicked things he was doing to her body were having an effect far beyond anything her imagination had ever conjured happening between man and wife.

"That's it... God you're beautiful. Come for me Eleanor."

Come? She was already there... right there... her hips lifted as she cried out again, her body arching with the exquisite release of tension as her body hummed with pleasure, tremors rocking through her.

Something inside of her stretched painfully, jabbing sharply through her core and Eleanor's eyes flew open to meet Edwin's above her. His weight came partially down on her as he lowered himself to his forearms and... he was inside of her! The high state of pleasure she had been dwelling in dimmed slightly as she realized this was not where she had meant this night to go.

"Wait!" she cried out, her hands coming up to push at his chest.

Misunderstanding her, thinking her reluctance a product of her innocent state, Edwin kissed the base of her slim throat. "It will only hurt for a moment sweetheart, try to relax."

His hips flexed and moved forward, sinking the full length of his rod into her tight hole, feeling the slight resistance of her virginity give way easily to his turgid staff. Dear God but she was exquisitely snug, her body tightening and loosening around him as she adjusted to the new dimensions of her womanhood. It was extremely hard not to move but he contented himself with being surrounded by her wet warmth as she accustomed herself to his presence inside of her.

Kissing her softly, Edwin brushed away the tear at her cheek.

"It doesn't hurt too badly does it sweetheart?" he asked, his voice sincerely concerned. After all, he certainly didn't want her to end up with an aversion to their marriage bed.

"No, no, it doesn't hurt too badly," she reassured him automatically, touched by his attention to her. It truly didn't either, she was already adjusting to the sensation but... "I just... I didn't think..."

"Don't worry sweetheart." Edwin cut her off with a kiss to her lips, sensuous and compelling, so much more intimate now that they were actually joined together by flesh. "It will feel good, I'll make sure of it."

That wasn't what she meant, what she wanted, but the tiny moment of despair over his misunderstanding gave way to the most spectacular sensation as he began to move inside of her. Gasping, Eleanor clung to his bare shoulders, surprised at the silky feeling of his skin beneath her fingertips, and even more shocked by her body's urge to move with him, her hips seeming to have a mind of their own as she rocked beneath his smooth strokes.

The invasion was intimate, sensual, and breathtakingly pleasurable. Her body was still humming from the spectacular release he'd driven her to with his mouth and hands, making her much more aware of the area between her legs than she'd ever been before. Edwin's lips coaxed hers open beneath his, his tongue exploring the insides of her mouth as he continued to move inside of her body in a much more explicit way, his hands roaming over her body and inflaming her passions.

The feel of his wife moving beneath him, her inner thighs rubbing against the outsides of his legs as she writhed in pleasure, the small mewling sounds she made in the back of her throat as he kissed her deeply, was driving Edwin absolutely wild. While he'd fantasized about Eleanor more than once since watching her birching, he hadn't expected such an explosive union as this or even suspected at how her innocent responses would inflame his desire for her.

Every inch of his manhood was encased in tight silken snugness, wetted with her honey, the taste of which still lingered on his tongue. Her body was soft beneath his, welcoming, and her reluctance seemed to have completely fallen away under his erotic assault on her senses. Burying himself inside of her, he groaned as her muscles squeezed his rod tightly, rippling around him as she moaned and squirmed delightfully.

Moving purposefully he drew gasps of pleasure from her, building up the inferno of her passions again, using his nimble fingers to rub between their bodies and tweak her sensitive pearl. Eleanor gasped and heaved beneath him, her legs wrapping around the backs of his thighs as she took him deeper. Her throaty cries of rapture as she climaxed pushed him over the edge and he thrust deep and hard, filling her completely as he shot spurt after spurt of potent seed into her body, completing their consummation.

She could actually feel him pulsing against her inner walls, feel the hot fluid spurting inside of her, and Eleanor shuddered around him in abject ecstasy as her body throbbed in response. Their mutual moans and caresses lifted and then slowed, Edwin's weight settling onto her in an intimate embrace.

Eleanor's heart pounded as her breathing slowed and she felt completely flummoxed. Nothing in her life had prepared her for a husband. Not even the warnings clamoring in her body when Edwin had stirred her interest had even hinted at the wonder and glories to be found in a man's bed. She hadn't had a chance once he'd started his seduction, and now there was no way to even consider annulling the marriage.

On the other hand, despite the fact that her father had arranged her future, Eleanor found she was feeling just a little bit less resistant to it.

"Ah Eleanor," Edwin breathed as he kissed the side of her neck and slid off of her, gathering her into his arms. To her surprise, she found she rather enjoyed his embrace, even though her desire to couple with him had already been satisfied. "That was wonderful."

"It truly was," she said, sounding high and breathless and not at all like herself. Then again she'd never felt quite like this before in her life. She didn't quite know what else to say, but fortunately Edwin didn't seem interested in further conversation. Sliding off to the side of her, he curled his muscular body around her softer one, holding her against him in an almost comforting manner.

Feeling rather confused, she drifted off to sleep in his arms.

CHAPTER 3

hen Eleanor awoke she was alone in her bed and she wasn't sure whether or not to feel disappointed. The tousled sheets beside her were proof she had not spent the night alone, as was the small spatter of blood beneath her, and she realized she felt rather sore in a rather delicious way. But she had slept in later than she'd meant to. Her maid Bridget helped her bathe and dress in a blue muslin morning dress that brought out the color of her eyes before she went down to breakfast where her husband was waiting. The moment she saw Edwin, so handsomely attired and looking more attractive than ever now that she knew exactly what pleasures he could give her, Eleanor blushed.

But Edwin just smiled at her and greeted her warmly. During breakfast he asked her to plan a dinner party for them and to think about where she might like to go for a wedding trip; they wouldn't leave for several weeks as he hadn't had time to make arrangements before their hasty union. It was quite a reasonable explanation but Eleanor found herself reminded of how she hadn't had the wedding she'd always dreamed of and now she had to wait for her honeymoon? And plan a dinner party in the mean time?

"Don't pout, sweetheart," Edwin said amiably as he rose. "I'll make it up to you when we go. I'm sure we can find ways to enjoy ourselves in the meantime."

Heat rose in her cheeks again as she realized what ways he was hinting at. That thought distracted her as her husband gave her a kiss on the cheek and left to attend to his business.

Then she got angry all over again. The nerve of the man! Not only had she been forced into a marriage she hadn't wanted, but then he'd used his... his... *wiles* on her—wiles probably practiced on many a lady —and seduced her inexperienced and ill-prepared self into his bed, and then the very next morning had the audacity to assign her a chore in the form of a dinner party! All the while going about his normal business of the day as if he hadn't just gotten married the day before.

Although, of course, they didn't need time to get to know each other as they had known each other for most of their lives, but still. Thinking about the wedding and honeymoon she had been dreaming of since she was a little girl and now had been denied, Eleanor felt incensed all over again. Plan a dinner party? For that insufferable lout? Ha!

Instead Eleanor's mind turned to the trousseau she was quite sure she deserved, especially considering her hasty wedding and delayed wedding trip. Well. That was something she could certainly begin to plan today, starting with the kinds of dresses she'd always wanted to wear.

WHEN EDWIN RETURNED HOME LATER that afternoon, pleased with the amount of work he'd gotten done during the day while still allowing him time to attend to his wife, he was rather disgruntled to be informed Eleanor had left soon after he had in the morning and so far had not returned. Perhaps she had gone to visit her family? After all, that would certainly be understandable considering their wedding had happened rather hastily. It would not be surprising if she did not feel comfortable in her new surroundings yet. Feeling less displeased and more indulgent he retired to his study so he could continue setting his estates and affairs in order before their honeymoon. After all, Eleanor had not been the only one ill prepared for such a hasty union.

Several hours later Edwin was informed by the butler that Lady Hyde had returned home. Checking his pocket watch, Edwin frowned and ordered her maid be called to his study. Had Eleanor really spent all day at her parent's house? Somehow, knowing Eleanor's nature, he did not think so.

Displeasure returned when he was duly informed of his wife's activities.

Shopping. Quite a bit of it in fact, spending a ridiculous amount of blunt on his accounts. Granted, he had not given her an amount for an allowance as of yet, but then she had not mentioned she would be shopping today. Why had she gone shopping, spending an irresponsible amount of money to buy herself an entirely new wardrobe when she already had a suitable one, rather than getting to know the staff or familiarizing herself with the household?

Here he had assigned the most innocent of motives to her day long absence only to find she had indulged in her most willfully spoiled behavior, thinking of no one but herself. Apparently the time under her father's tutelage was not enough to counteract the many years of being spoiled by her mother which had come before that. A flicker of excitement ran through him, shunting aside his frustration, when he realized this was the perfect time to enact the discipline with which he would punish his wife when she acted so thoughtlessly... although, of course, he would allow her time to attempt and explain her actions first.

Feeling both excited and generous, Edwin told the maid to send his wife to meet him.

Heart pounding in his chest, he realized part of him hoped Eleanor *had* reverted back to her spoiled self so he could justifiably take her over his knee. Although their wedding night had been quite passionate and delightful, satisfying those urges had not stopped his desire for more unusual ways in which to take pleasure in his wife's delightful body. He quite yearned to redden her bottom, but it wouldn't be nearly as satisfying unless the discipline was truly necessary.

~

SUMMONED TO HER HUSBAND, Eleanor swept coolly into the study, all the while feeling smugly satisfied at the wonderful revenge she'd had on him today. Her shopping excursion had borne much fruit. She'd ordered items her father would never have allowed her, due to the expense, as well as being measured for gowns much more mature and colorful than the demure pastels she'd had to wear as a debutante, and the other beautiful fripperies she'd yearned for but would never have dared buy all at once. Spending Edwin's money on her heart's desires had been monumentally satisfying. That would teach him.

"Eleanor, it has come to my attention I have been remiss in attending to matters with you," Edwin said in a conciliatory tone. Hiding a smile, Eleanor lifted her head high, ready to graciously receive his apologies for whatever wrongs he'd finally realized he'd done her. She was quite sure he wouldn't have recognized all of them right away, but perhaps he'd realized she shouldn't have been left completely alone on their first day as a married couple. Or he should have insisted to her father that she have a proper wedding. Or for marrying her at all. "But there is no time like the present to set matters to right. You have quite overspent on the allowance you will be issued each month. In fact, if your maid's memory was correct, then you have overspent on almost a year's worth of allowance. Therefore I hope you bought everything you needed today for you will not be allowed to purchase any more items for yourself until next year." She gaped as his tone turned quite severe and fury flashed through her.

"Perhaps I would not have overspent if my new husband had deigned to spend the day in my company."

To her surprise, Edwin's countenance darkened as if he was angry at her retort rather than ashamed at his behavior.

"Unlike you, I have spent the day working, putting the necessary affairs in order for a wedding trip, while you have been out spending enough blunt that I'm not sure we'll be able to do everything I would have liked. Unlike you, everything I have done today has been to benefit both of us, more specifically to set my affairs in order so I might have the time to spend with you. This marriage was as unexpected for me as it was for you. As I told you at breakfast. If you had informed me at breakfast of your intentions for the day, then I would have told you what your allowance was. Even so, I can't understand what on earth you would need an entirely new wardrobe for when I know you had received one for your coming out. Several dresses as befitting your new status as my wife would have been reasonable, an entirely new selection is not."

Edwin approached her, his words slicing through her arguments. As he came closer she found herself noticing the way his broad shoulders filled his coat, his dark eyes flashing, and the uncompromising set of his strongly delineated jaw. It was both fascinating and frightening as he crowded her space but she found herself unable to move or back away, too taken aback by his accusations and her own culpability.

"Furthermore, when I left you at breakfast you did not protest my leave-taking or give any hint to the fact that you were put out about my plans for the day. I will not take the blame for not being able to discern your thoughts without a word from you."

Staring up at her husband, Eleanor's jaw worked soundlessly, only now realizing that her temper had perhaps been a bit impetuous and she had not conducted herself in a very becoming or rational manner. But she hadn't expected such censure from Edwin either. This was not the similarly impetuous youth she'd known as her brother's friend. The stormily attractive man in front of her was much more imposing, much more threatening.

So she took a page from her own book in dealing with her mother and thrust her lower lip out in a pout.

"I should not have had to tell you. Anyone with sense should have realized a bride does not wish to be abandoned the day after her wedding. And a poor excuse for a wedding at that. No flowers, no noble guests, I didn't even have a proper dress." She let tears begin to leak from her eyes, staring up at him imploringly. "I am a married lady now and I wanted a married lady's wardrobe, I should not have to keep dressing like a debutante. Only a brute would treat me the way you are now!"

How did she manage to still look beautiful while crying? Ah, but these were not real tears. Edwin had not missed the calculation in her eyes —and he remembered what she had looked like after her birching when the tears she had shed had been quite real. These were nothing more than water from her beautiful blue eyes.

Hardening his heart to her spoiled manipulations, Edwin grabbed her by the arm and pulled her over to the chair. Sitting down in it he yanked her across his lap, his heart beating madly as he prepared to spank his wife. His real anger warred with his excitement over the much anticipated event.

"What are you doing?" she screeched, any pretense at hurt feelings or tears forgotten as she was hauled over his knee, spitting mad.

"I am teaching you a lesson," he said calmly, although he felt anything but calm. Screeching, Eleanor tried to push herself up but he grabbed her wrists and held them in the small of her back, hooking his leg around hers and pressing them between his own calf and the leg of the chair. Tipping her forward so her bottom was high in the air, her face pressed between his thigh and the arm of the chair, Edwin used his free hand to lift her skirts.

"How dare you?!" she yelled, although he could also hear the touch of fear in her voice. With her soft body across him, her anxiety heightening, his own desire was beginning to pulse through his veins and he could feel himself hardening against her stomach. "Unhand me this instant! This is not how you treat a wife!"

"No, this is how I treat a spoiled child," he said, tucking her skirts around her waist as he began to lower her drawers. They, unfortunately, had a sewed in-seam. Well as long as he was buying her new clothing, he would make sure to buy some of those as well. "A spoiled child who spends without a thought for the future, who is more concerned with her wedding than her marriage, who does not tell her husband she wishes his company and then punishes him for her own lack of communication, and who then dissembles and produces false tears in an attempt to shame him, rather than admit her own short-comings and apologize."

Finally her drawers were down to her knees, revealing the creamy expanse of her bottom and thighs. Edwin's cock pulsed. He was certainly going to have to buy her some of the old fashioned kind, like the ones she'd been wearing when she'd been birched; he would love to have her spread her legs when he spanked her so he could see her cunny better, adding to the vulnerability of the punishment, but with her drawers around her knees that wouldn't be possible.

Ignoring her alternating demands and pleas, Edwin raised his hand and brought it down hard on her right cheek, leaving a red hand print as Eleanor yelped and shrieked.

"That's one," he said, watching as her skin turned a light pink color after the initial red spank. Rubbing his hand over the spot, his loins felt fit to burst already. "I will give you the chance to apologize for your thoughtlessness and selfishness after twenty or another twenty will be added."

"Let me up!"

"Two." His hand came down just as hard on her other cheek and Eleanor yelped.

While he was quite sure the birching he'd witnessed her being given had not been the last she's received, taking a spanking from her husband seemed to be having a most salutary effect on his new wife. She shrieked and yelped, but she had ceased to struggle, lying in his lap and accepting his punishment as he laid down smack after smack on the rounded globes of her buttocks, turning them a rosy pink. Since it was her first spanking, he was careful not to use full force. After all, while she was used to such discipline from her father, this was obviously not what she had expected from a marriage—and certainly not from him—and he wanted to ease her into it. As long as she didn't do anything too terrible. Really she deserved a harder spanking than he was giving her, but he was inclined towards being gentler for this first time.

"Three."

"Edwin, please!"

"Four."

"Damn you!"

She let out a louder scream as his next two hits came down with more force. After all, he couldn't allow her to think that cursing him was acceptable. "Five. Six."

By ten she was begging to apologize and Edwin paused for a moment, letting his hand rub across her bright pink bottom.

"I am punishing you, not coercing you. You will take the full twenty as punishment and then you will have the opportunity to apologize, but the apology does not diminish your punishment."

His hand raised again. "Eleven."

Concentrating all the force of his blows on two spots on her buttocks, one on each cheek, Edwin deliberately hit them over and over again so she would be feeling the effects every time she sat down for some time afterwards. Her bottom was turning rosy red amidst cream, inflaming his desires further as she squirmed against him and he wondered if she could feel his arousal as it pressed against her. His breeches felt uncommonly tight as the enjoyment of spanking his wife seemed to have stretched his pego to monstrous proportions.

"Twenty."

On his lap, Eleanor quivered as she cried.

Putting his hand on one flaming red buttock, Edwin nearly groaned at the heat beneath his palm. Spanking his wife had been so much more satisfying than any previous disciplinary experience he'd ever had. Eleanor not only deserved the spanking but her bottom looked so beautiful all hot and red. Having her on his lap made a very large difference, especially as she'd physically stopped fighting him quite quickly despite her verbal protests and pleas. There was certainly something to be said for a wife who was already accustomed to this kind of discipline.

48

He caressed her beaten bottom, his fingers brushing across the glossy, wet curls of her cunt... wait... wet? Shocked and even more aroused, Edwin dipped his hand down to her cunny and his wife moaned, trying to burrow her head down into the armchair as he found evidence of her own arousal. The slickness of Eleanor's slit was both shocking and arousing. But this was supposed to be punishment after all, not pleasure.

Clearing his throat, Edwin pushed his wife up from his lap, taking note of her red rimmed puffy eyes, the blotchy cheeks and quivering lower lip. Yes, *that* was what Eleanor looked like when she actually cried. Her blonde hair was slightly disordered now, making her look younger and even more vulnerable. Still he couldn't help but enjoy the sight of her blonde muff, exposed by the set of her skirts, and the way her puckered nipples were pressing against the front of her dress. However, he intended to enjoy the sight of her backside for the next few minutes.

"Go stand in the corner with your skirts around your waist so I can see your bottom and you think about how you'd like to apologize. I will give you five minutes. After that you will make your apology or you'll go back over my lap."

TRUTHFULLY, if Eleanor hadn't been so shocked and ashamed at her reaction to her husband's high handedness and punishment she might not have gone so quietly to the corner as he ordered, but she was in a bit of a daze. Never in her life had she expected something like that to occur. Nose to the corner, skirts in her hands, with a burning bottom was nothing new to her, despite her antipathy to the position, but she'd never been *aroused* under such circumstances before.

Then again, the last person to take her across their *lap* for a spanking was her governess when she was nine. It was quite different being hauled across the muscular thighs of her damnably attractive husband, his body holding her in place, his broad hand coming down hard on her soft, vulnerable flesh, and the turgid length of his rod pressing into her stomach. But he hadn't seemed the least bit ashamed of it, nor had he acted on it, whereas she could not countenance her own reaction.

It had not been the pain that had made her sob and beg, after all she'd taken harder spankings before, but she'd been so ashamed at her feelings of excitement under the circumstances, not to mention the helplessness of her position and the vulnerability and embarrassment of her husband seeing her in such straights. Never in her life had she expected something like that to happen to her and now, as she was standing in the corner, she found her anger growing that Edwin would handle her thus and force such unnatural sensations on her. And after the beauty of last night too!

Her cheeks blushed hotly as she realized her womanhood was just as slick now as it had been last night, and Edwin was well aware of the fact. For once she was glad to be in the corner, glad her reddened bottom was facing him so she didn't have to look at him and see his expression.

Lost in her thoughts and humiliation, the five minutes passed incredibly quickly and Eleanor found herself being ordered to turn around. He did not allow her to lower her skirts, so she was forced to make her apology with her skirts around her waist and her drawers around her ankles. Lowering her eyes rather than facing him, she did her best to hide her shame and fury as she stammered out an apology. To her relief, Edwin accepted it.

And then had the audacity to sweep her up in his arms for a passionate kiss, probing the depths of her mouth with his tongue. Forgetting herself, Eleanor responded to him, her hands clutching at the fabric filling her hands, forgetting she was holding onto her skirts until she felt his fingers curve over her bare bottom. Then his hand gripped her soft, red flesh, hard, and she cried out as the hard grip reignited the sting in her buttocks.

Immediately Eleanor wriggled away, dropping her skirts in the process. She quickly reached beneath them to pull up her drawers, refusing to look at Edwin as her face turned as red as her bottom with embarrassment. Why could she not control her own body around him?

"I'll see you at dinner, seven o'clock, sharp," said her husband, his tone making it clear he expected her to be there on time.

Eleanor mumbled something and quit the room, almost running in her anxiety to leave her punishment, inexplicable reaction, and subsequent humiliation behind.

EDWIN THOUGHT the first attempt at domestic discipline had gone rather well. Not only had Eleanor submitted to the spanking but she'd actually become aroused by it. Once she was gone from his study he rather regretted not taking advantage of the moment and pleasuring them both, thereby relieving the throbbing erection the spanking had induced, but considering her general confusion when she'd left, he felt perhaps he'd made the correct choice. After all, she was already dealing with quite a lot between being married yesterday and having her first spanking at the hands of her husband today. Considering how happy he already was with the match, he was inclined to be magnanimous.

However, sitting behind his desk he found it impossible to return to his work. Images of Eleanor kept rising in his mind; her delightful bottom with the red prints of his hands on either cheek, the wonderful feel of her squirming on his lap, her rosy bottom on display in the corner, and the way she'd responded to him when he'd kissed her. He had meant to wait until later tonight, to spend his pleasure in his wife, but he found his libido was not inclined to be ruled by his intentions.

Retrieving his handkerchief from his pocket he undid the front of his breeches and took his throbbing rod in hand, feeling the aching pulse of its rigid length against his palm. Closing his eyes, he leaned back in his chair as he began to fist himself, the silky material of the handkerchief rubbing against the plum of his cock in the most delicious fashion as he relived the events of the past twenty minutes. The feel of Eleanor's soft arse quivering beneath his palm, the heat of her reddened skin, and the surprising wetness of her womanly folds following her punishment.

With a low groan he squeezed his aching member hard, and it pulsed and jerked as it spewed forth cream into the handkerchief.

Humming happily, he discarded the handkerchief and got back to work. More than ever he wanted to finish setting his matters at rest so he could take Eleanor on a wedding trip.

~

SAFELY ENSCONCED IN HER ROOM, Eleanor lay on her stomach on the bed, hating the slight burn in her bottom that reminded her with every movement of her husband. Although he had made several admittedly fair points during his lecture to her, Eleanor resented the punishment and especially resented how it had aroused feelings of desire in her. It was so unfair.

Not only was she saddled with a husband she hadn't wanted, even if she did find him inordinately attractive, with a dismal excuse for a wedding, but now even her own body had betrayed her. Shame and the lack of satisfaction for the need pulsing between her legs gave way to another bout of tears as she considered her options. After last night, an annulment was out of the question. Running away was not a real option either; who would she go to? No one in her family would help her when her father had been the one to set the match. Without a relative to provide succor, she would have to work.

Eleanor shuddered. Absolutely unacceptable for someone of her bloodlines and noble rank to be forced to work. Besides, the only positions she would be fit for were governess or companion and neither of those positions would allow for the finer things in life.

Perhaps she could convince her husband to allow her to stay with a friend? Perhaps Lady Grace... she certainly would understand troubles between a husband and a wife. Convincing a friend to hide her away would mean foregoing the balls and parties she so enjoyed, but if Edwin were amenable... Eleanor made a face. Somehow she didn't think her husband would be all that amenable. Despite the fact they had known each other for years before their marriage yesterday, Edwin was showing facets of himself she had never suspected existed; however, she'd always known of his stubbornness and his sense of dignity. It was highly doubtful he'd let his new bride live with someone else so early in their marriage, it would cause too much gossip.

Maybe she could frustrate and annoy him to the point where he would be desirous of foisting her off onto someone else. While such a plan might get her bottom reddened a few more times, surely he would cease and desist when he realized how little of an effect such discipline had on her? The only reason she'd ever acquiesced to her father's demands was because she knew she would soon escape his household and it was only for a short period of time, and her father had had a much heavier hand than Edwin. She could certainly with-stand a few more bouts of Edwin's discipline, knowing that disobeying was actually furthering her own goals.

Now if only she could convince her newly awakened passions that separating from her husband was a good idea.

"My lady?" Her maid, Poppy, came into the room, frowning a little to see her mistress laid out on the bed. "Would you like me to help you dress for dinner?"

Seven o'clock sharp? A small smile curved Eleanor's lips as she realized this was the perfect start to defying her husband and ulti-mately gaining her freedom. Such a small thing, denying him her presence when he'd ordered it, so soon after discipline would both be subtle and send the undeniable message that his punishment hadn't quite had the effect he'd intended.

"I am not feeling at all the thing, Poppy," she said smoothly. "Help me out of this dress and into my night rail and then have Cook send a tray up to my room. I will dine here tonight."

CHAPTER 4

*E*dwin dismissed the maid from his room, frowning as he looked in his mirror. Tonight he'd tried to dress to please Eleanor and yet here she was defying him again. Was she truly ill or was this a fit of pique? Or even another attempt at manipulation? He certainly wouldn't put it past her, but as a fair minded man he did want to give her the benefit of the doubt.

The past forty-eight hours had been full of many shocks after all, and even if part of him suspected Eleanor was currently far too self-engrossed to really be dented by any of those shocks, that didn't mean he was necessarily correct. There were other facets to her personality as well, it was just that being indulged had created some less admirable qualities in her.

Turning to Johnson, his valet, he tugged off the cravat he'd just had put on, ignoring the man's sigh of dissatisfaction at his employer's state of attire. "Go tell Mrs. Hester I will bring the tray to my wife and to put enough food for two on it."

If Eleanor was truly unwell then Edwin would sit up with her and do what he could, including keeping her company. If she wasn't unwell… well they wouldn't be leaving her bedchamber for some time anyway and having the food there would be fortuitous.

54

Humming softly under his breath, Edwin found himself hoping for the latter.

~

WHEN THE DOOR to her bedroom opened, Eleanor waved her hand at the table beside her.

"You can put the tray here," she said not looking up from her book. It was comfortable in front of the fire, curled up in the chair, and warm enough that she'd loosened her robe in the front so it gaped open slightly.

"You don't look very ill to me," said a deep voice as the tray settled next to her.

With a gasp, Eleanor's head jerked upwards to meet the censuring eyes of her husband. Edwin looked darkly handsome, as always, wearing nothing more than a pair of trousers and a loose shirt open at the neck, showing a hint of his muscular chest and a few curly hairs peeking out. Apprehension and excitement curdled through her at the hot and lustful anger in his eyes, so similar to how he'd looked at her this afternoon.

What was wrong with her?

"What are you doing here?" she asked, her voice coming out sharper than she'd intended because of her trepidation over her body's reaction to him.

"Well right now I'm wondering what you're doing in here, instead of down at the dinner table with me."

Eleanor tilted her chin upwards, well aware the effect was diminished with him standing over her, but she was so used to assuming the haughty posture when she was being defiant that it was automatic.

"I was feeling ill."

"Are you still feeling ill?"

"Yes."

"You don't look ill," he said, repeating his earlier statement as she glared up at him.

"Looking at you is making me feel sick to my stomach," she

snapped rudely. Sighing, Edwin shook his head and turned and walked away. For a moment, a surge of triumph went through her, but inexplicably he stopped and sat on her bed. "What are you doing?"

"Lying to me is unacceptable," Edwin said calmly, watching her from his place on the bed. "So is disrespect. Neither shall be tolerated. Since this is the first time we've talked this though I will go easy on you, although both of those infractions should have been obvious."

A frisson of unease shot through Eleanor. "I don't understand, what are you talking about?"

"Come," Edwin said, patting his lap. "Lay across my lap. You're due for another spanking."

"What?! No!" Although she'd set out to provoke her husband, she hadn't seriously considered he would spank her again so soon. The whole point had been to show him that his spanking hadn't had a real effect on her. "You've already beaten me enough today, don't you think?"

"I did not beat you," he said firmly, frowning at her with a glint of real anger in his eyes at her accusation. Even angry he looked so handsome that he nearly took her breath away. "You were not harmed in any way, you were disciplined for bad behavior. Since you are still exhibiting such behavior I am going to discipline you again. Now come here, take off your robe and lay across my lap. The longer you take to follow my orders the longer your spanking is going to last."

For a moment Eleanor considered further resistance but her goal was to provoke her husband into not wanting her presence anymore, not into giving her harsher punishments. She would show him; she would take the spanking and then continue her campaign tomorrow as if nothing had happened. Obviously the message hadn't gotten across yet, but after a few more disciplinary sessions with no change in her behavior and he'd realize spankings didn't work on her. Then she'd suggest she go stay with a friend and he'd be happy to see the back of her.

Still, it was harder than she'd expected to stand up and take off her robe, leaving it on the chair behind her. However, she couldn't stop the feminine thrill at the heat surging in Edwin's eyes and the way his pants bulged as she walked towards him in nothing but her thin night rail. Moving stiffly and reluctantly Eleanor came to stand in front him.

"Good girl," he crooned, taking her hand and pulling her down towards him. His hands on her made her shiver. "Now put your head on this side... yes that's it, and legs on this side..." The night rail was lifted so her bottom was exposed, still slightly pink from the spanking she'd received earlier that afternoon. "Now spread your legs."

The position was incredibly vulnerable, with her upper body on one side of his legs and her legs on the other, her bottom tilted upwards over his lap, and now he wanted her to spread her legs? "Do it now Eleanor. I told you, the longer you take, the longer your punishment will take."

A sharp slap to her thigh made her shiver and slowly she complied, burying her head into the coverlet on her bed as tears of shame sprang to her eyes. While she'd had to spread her legs for the occasional birchings she'd received in the past, this was a much more intimate humiliation. Already she'd found there was a great difference between bending over a chair and bending over a man's lap, especially a man such as Edwin. His hand caressed her bottom in an almost loving manner, exploring the rose and cream skin, and Eleanor bit back a moan, not wanting him to know this vulnerable and helpless position was arousing her, and certainly not wanting him to know the complex storm of emotions that accompanied his touch.

BEAUTIFUL. The hand prints he'd left on each cheek had faded somewhat, leaving only the slightest pink glow on her creamy skin. This position over his lap with her legs spread made her much more open to punishment than having her over his lap with her legs together. The night rail bunched around her waist only drew more attention to the delightful globes of her ass, the open leg position exposing her dusky bottom hole and pink cunny with its fringe of damp curls. He could see, quite clearly, that dew was already gathering on her petals.

Something about being punished by him appealed to her as much as it did to him. This was a much more exposed position, to both his eyes and his hand, and Edwin's pulse raced as his cock throbbed against her stomach for the second time that day.

Especially because he already knew he had no intention of denying himself the pleasure of spending in her body after this punishment.

"Why are you being punished Eleanor?" he asked, wanting to draw out this moment, to enjoy the feel of her body on his lap and the sight of her unprotected and waiting bottom, the pink shell of her cunt just below. Besides, it was best to ensure she knew exactly which behaviors she was being punished for.

"For lying." Her voice was tight and resentful, but he decided not to add to her punishment for that now. One step at a time and it was good she was answering him.

"And?"

"For being disrespectful." Not that her current tone of voice was at all respectful. But time enough later on to work on the small things, for now he would focus on punishing her for the larger transgressions.

"Good. One." His hand came down hard on the same spot he'd spanked earlier. "Two." He hit the other cheek on the same spot. "Three." Now his hand began to wander. Because this was her second spanking of the day and the nature of her transgressions Edwin had decided it should be a little more punitive, especially considering how long it had taken her to get into position. Forty should do it.

By ten Eleanor was crying again, her muffled gasps into the bed only serving to arouse him further. Her bottom was turning a delightful shade of rosy pink and slowly darkening as he spread the punitive slaps across its creamy surface. Firmly he brought spanks eleven and twelve down on the sensitive skin of the underside of her buttocks, right in the crease between her cheeks and thigh, and Eleanor shrieked, her legs starting to close a bit to protect herself.

"Open," he said, giving two sharp smacks to her inner thighs and she yelped and spread again. Another slap landed on her rump. "Thirteen."

"That should be fifteen! You just gave me two on my thighs!"

"That was to keep you in position, not part of this punishment," he said firmly, pressing down more firmly with his forearm, which was laid along the length of her back to keep her in position as she started to try and squirm away. The movement rubbed against his erect pego and he had to stifle a moan. A glance showed she was gripping the bed sheets with her hands; her bottom was already looking hot and each new slap must have stung quite a bit. Grinning, he landed another one on her rump, smacking a spot that looked a little bit less pink than the rest of her buttocks. "Fourteen."

Eleanor squirmed and bit at the sheets, yelping and crying as he spanked her, but she didn't try to get away again until he reached twenty.

"Twenty-one."

"No more! That's enough!" She wriggled, forcing him to haul her back into place.

"This is punishment, Eleanor. It's not for you to say when it's enough, it's for me." He was surprised to realize she obviously thought she would get no more than what he'd given her this afternoon. Still trying to control things. Had her father always kept the punishments the same or warned her beforehand if it was going to be different? Well, he thought to himself with a grin, she'd certainly have a time adjusting to his particular brand of discipline. He much preferred the idea of keeping things interesting.

Again he gave two hard smacks to her thighs, making her squeal as his hand came down hard on the tender skin, pink splotches appearing immediately. "Stay still and I will finish your punishment."

Now the sobbing began in earnest as she pleaded with him, her cries for mercy only arousing him further. Really her bottom wasn't even red yet, just a nice shade of dark pink. Going by the birching he'd witnessed a few years ago he knew she'd had much worse from her father. Perhaps she thought to manipulate him into being less harsh with her.

When he reached thirty he smacked the sensitive skin in the crease between her buttocks, allowing his fingers to slap against her exposed crinkled hole and Eleanor shrieked her loudest yet, trying to jerk upwards against his forearm, but he held her firmly in place. As he landed another smack in the same location she screeched and began to close her legs again in an attempt to protect the sensitive nerves bundled there. Edwin immediately stopped spanking her.

"Spread your legs immediately Eleanor or we'll start all over again," he said in a tone that brooked no argument.

Sniffling Eleanor complied. The soft skin along her crease looked red and puffy and Edwin avoided it for a few more slaps before laying another one down her crack. She cried out and squirmed but kept her legs open, and so Edwin rewarded her by making the last blow to her cheek rather than down the center, although he filed the knowledge away for later. With her punishment was over, Edwin caressed her buttocks gently, soothing the ache that must be in them. His hand dipped lower and lower over her hot skin as she mewled and pressed her head down into the bed as if embarrassed.

When he reached her quim he understood why. Eleanor was aroused, very aroused going by the substantial amount of cream coating her folds. Sopping wet. He groaned as he plunged his fingers into her hot core and she wriggled on his lap, trying to escape the intrusion of his fingers, but Edwin just held her firmly as he began to push them back and forth inside of her, mimicking what he wanted to be doing with his cock. God his wife was a treasure; not only used to a firm hand of discipline, but apparently as heated by it as he was.

As he fingered her, enjoying the soft squelching noises of her wet pussy and the whimpering moans emitting from her lips, he continued to caress her hot cheeks with his other hand, squeezing slightly and enjoying her sounds of protest as his firm grip reignited the pain from her punishment.

Finally he couldn't take it any longer. Removing his hand from her wetness, he pulled her night rail over her head before practically tossing her onto the bed.

"Edwin!" she said in a shocked tone as she turned to look at him. Edwin was already divesting himself of his clothing as she stared up at him with something approaching horror. "You can't... we can't possibly..."

He snorted. "Don't try to tell me you don't want it wife, you're soaking wet."

Heat flushed her cheeks and she tried to scoot away from him. Although he had undone the front of his trousers he hadn't pulled them off yet; he crawled onto the bed after her, grabbing her ankle and enjoying the view of her naked body. Between her legs her pink lips glistened, the blonde hair framing it was slightly darker with her juices and her rosy nipples were erect and begging for attention.

"But you just punished me!" she cried out, turning on her stomach in an attempt to crawl away. Unfortunately for her, that movement only inflamed him further as her red bottom was turned back to him and he decided on the spot that he wanted to take his wife in dog-fashion so he could enjoy the view of her disciplined cheeks.

"And I know how much we both enjoyed it," he said ruthlessly, grabbing her hips and pulling them upwards. Eleanor cried out, obviously not understanding what was going on as she looked over her shoulder at him in consternation. Well, she was about to find out.

Edwin placed the head of his cock at her dripping cunny and her eyes got even bigger as she tried to twist away. "What are you doing?! This isn't how a husband makes love to his wife!"

"A husband may make love to his wife in any way he pleases," Edwin said and he thrust forward to prove his point, skewering her on his rampant cock. "And this husband pleases to make love to his disobedient wife in this fashion so he can admire his handiwork. If you do not enjoy it then I suggest you try to behave in the future."

Although part of him thought that more lecturing might do her some good he was too distracted by the incredible sensation of her wet, sucking heat as he began to thrust back and forth into her protesting body. Eleanor continued to protest, but her pleas were interspersed with soft moans of pleasure as he took her hard and fast, enjoying the sight of his cock burying itself in her welcoming quim, her quivering red buttocks bouncing every time he slammed into her from behind. At this point he could tell her protests were token, she was bucking and moving back against him with pleasure, her muscles tightening around him as he rode her hard. There was absolutely no question of whether or not she liked it, although she might not *want* to.

Enjoying his wife's slow submission to her desires, Edwin decided to help her along. Leaning forward he reached beneath her body to cup her breasts, squeezing them tightly and using them to leverage her body back into his. When he pinched her nipples between his fingers and began to roll them back and forth she bucked and mewled, her pussy convulsing around him with pleasure.

"I know you like this," he panted in her ear. "I can feel your hot quim gripping me and the heat of your ass against my stomach. I've had dreams of you for years and now you're mine... all mine..." Granted, his dreams had been about the birching he'd witnessed, but it was true that in his marriage to her, all of his dreams seemed to be coming true.

"Please..." she begged. "Please..."

"Please what?" he asked, fucking her harder, his hips moving faster as his excitement over the spanking and her creamy tunnel began to peak. "Please stop? Please don't stop?" One hand released a breast and slid down her stomach to press against her engorged pearl, rubbing the slick little bud firmly and she cried out, her back arching with pleasure.

"Please... Edwin... Oh Edwin... don't stop...!"

And then she screamed and her tight tunnel spasmed around him, massaging his thrusting cock. He could feel himself swelling inside of her just as her walls tightened down around him and he released her breast and pulled back, thrusting hard one final time to bury himself inside of her as deeply as possible, filling her with his seed. It felt like she was sucking every last drop from him with her tight sheathe, her high cries softening to moans as her own climax abated. Holding himself inside of her, he caressed her bottom some more, enjoying the way the aftershocks of her climax made her occasionally convulse around his slowly softening cock.

Although he remained half-hard, he eventually—reluctantly—

pulled himself from her body. Eleanor turned onto her side to look up at him, her expression full of confusion. He couldn't help but smile, part of him liked that his new wife was off balance with him. It kept things interesting. Planting a hand on either side of her head, he leaned down and kissed her thoroughly, enjoying the taste of her sweet lips and the fact that even now she responded to him.

When he finished the kiss he finished stripping off his trousers. He'd decided he wanted Eleanor to remain bare and therefore he would join her in her nakedness so she would not feel too embarrassed. Besides, if he decided to take her again then he might as well be ready.

So far none of her plans were coming to fruition.

Eleanor was quite shaken by this evening's turn of events. Not the discipline really, once Edwin had appeared in her room she had expected that. Although having him turn up had been a surprise. Especially since he had seemed legitimately concerned when he first walked in the room before he realized she was lying. Her reaction to being spanked by him, however, was increasingly disturbing. Being held over his lap was so intimate and so arousing, yet so very, very wrong.

That he had wanted to commence relations immediately following the act was even more wrong and yet she couldn't deny her embarrassing reaction to him. Or the immense pleasure which followed. Edwin had played her body skillfully, drawing her to a rousing conclusion that still made her cheeks heat with humiliation every time she thought about it.

And now they were having dinner together, naked, in her room as if nothing was out of the ordinary.

She had no idea what to do other than pretend everything was normal, despite the cooled food and their state of undress. They chatted and talked, and she did her best to ignore the way his eyes lingered on her exposed breasts. At least he couldn't see her lower half right now.

"Have you made any plans for the dinner party?" he asked.

"No." In fact plans had been the last thing on her mind today.

"I see." That was all he said, but his expression and tone held a volume of disapproval. Looking down at her plate, Eleanor moved the peas around with her fork. Although she wanted her husband to decide he was better off without her continued presence, she did not relish the idea of being punished again tonight. But all he said was, "I hope tomorrow you will have more time to devote to making plans."

"What's your favorite food?" she asked, quite suddenly, the seed of an idea forming in her mind. Edwin raised his eyebrow at her but he allowed her to change the topic to the kinds of food he was partial to and those he despised. The conversation seemed quite innocuous since she was planning a dinner party. He even made her laugh when he described his youthful attempts to avoid eating mashed turnips—hiding them in his napkin, feeding them to the dog, and the particularly scandalous time when he'd filled his pockets with the stuff only to be discovered when he'd left the table and it became evident that the moisture had seeped through the fabric of his trousers. Once the ice was broken it became a rather fun and interesting dinner and she discovered Edwin was just as easy to talk to, as when she had been a young girl.

It might have been perfect if only she wasn't naked. If her bottom wasn't so sore. And if she wasn't plotting something nefarious for the dinner party.

CHAPTER 5

For the next week, Eleanor considered herself on her best behavior. She also spent as much time as possible avoiding Edwin, other than mealtimes and bedtime when she couldn't avoid him at all. Underneath her pleasant demeanor, she was relishing her plans for the upcoming dinner party, although she had to admit it was much easier to be pleasant with Edwin than it was to be constantly biting at his heels. Even more pleasant were the hours they spent in bed, where she found herself becoming surprisingly addicted to his hands, his lips, and well... all the rest of him.

In her free time she visited with her friends and family, went to social engagements and did her best to fill her time away from the house. She'd managed to leave the majority of the running of the house to Mrs. Hester to avoid being home very often even though it was fairly easy to avoid Edwin when she was a home. He was very busy getting his affairs in order so they could go on their honeymoon.

On occasion, she would still merit a small spanking, usually for saying something disrespectful to him. But mostly Edwin was showing himself to be a rather amiable husband and there were times when she almost forgot she was trying to provoke him into accepting her idea to live separately.

Still, being married might not be so bad if she didn't have to ask him for everything. Other wives received allowances. And she didn't entirely believe him that she'd overspent on hers. After all, she knew very well from listening to his conversations with Hugh that Edwin was even more well off than her family and Momma spent whatever she pleased. Although, her mother had never bought an entirely new wardrobe in one day.

Soon Edwin would realize there was no point in chastising her and he would give up and allow her to go her own way, preferably to live at Lady Grace's house. She'd hinted to her mother that things with Edwin weren't going quite the way she wanted them to, but her mother seemed completely oblivious. Hugh was still courting Miss Chandler and the fathers were quietly negotiating, which was holding the majority of her mother's attention, and the rest of her conversation was spent praising Edwin. There would be no help or sympathy from either of her parents, it was clear.

EDWIN KNEW his wife was up to something. There was a little gleam of triumph in Eleanor's eye lately whenever she looked at him. In fact, he was letting a lot of little instances of bad behavior slide just because he wanted to see what she was saving up for. Curiosity was ruling him at the moment. Later he would have plenty of time to discipline her for the laziness with which she was performing her duties as lady of the house. Although he still reacted to insults or blatant disrespect with an immediate punishment, he had so far not chastised her for ignoring her duties.

Oh yes, he was well aware that the burden had fallen onto his housekeeper, who was really not supposed to be running the household anymore. And she wasn't happy about it either. Mrs. Hester had come to speak with him, hinting she was becoming frustrated with the current state of affairs. He'd soothed her and offered her a pay raise, and told her soon Lady Hyde would be taking up the reins of the household, as she was supposed to be doing. At least she'd finally gotten the invitations for the dinner party out and was mostly taking responsibility for planning that. It was a combination of both his and her friends, unfortunately, Wesley still wasn't back in England.

As soon as he found out what she was planning he would make sure she knew things would not continue the way they had been. He had a feeling it was going to make for a wonderful reason for punishment. And afterwards he'd have even more justification disciplining her for the smaller matters. In the meantime, it was delightful to have such a lovely and responsive wife in his bed, although he wished he saw more of her during the day. That was something else which was going to have to be fixed. She was always out gallivanting around without telling him where she was going or who she was spending her time with. When he asked in the evenings, he was fairly certain she wasn't being entirely truthful with him.

But he was somewhat distracted by business affairs and getting things in order before their honeymoon so he was letting a lot of little things slip by, like the fact he was fairly certain she was occasionally lying to him. Soon he'd be able to take care of that. Even when they returned home from their honeymoon, his time wouldn't be quite so taken up by business and so he would be able to attend more to her.

There was a knock on his study door and Edwin looked up from the current batch of accounts he was reviewing. After their honeymoon he'd have to take a visit to the estates. He wondered how Eleanor would take leaving London.

"Yes Banks?" he asked as his butler stepped into the room.

"Viscount Petersham is here to see you, my Lord." In his late forties, Banks had the usual starchy demeanor of a butler. He'd been with Edwin since Edwin had come to London, a stalwart presence who had seen him through several initial mishaps.

"Ah, Hugh, very good. You may send him in."

The door closed and Edwin shuffled the papers he had been looking at into the proper order. He liked to keep things neat on his desk, everything in its proper place. It only took him a few moments to have everything arranged as he liked it when Banks returned and admitted Hugh into the study.

Grinning, Edwin stood and walked around the desk to clasp his friend and brother-in-law's hand. Within five minutes they were lounging in his arm chairs, armed with glasses of brandy.

"So, how goes the married life?" asked Hugh. "You're still alive so I suppose that means Eleanor's behaving."

"She's up to something," said Edwin, a little anticipatory smile curving across his face.

Hugh shook his head. "And you're looking forward to whatever mad little scheme she has going through her head? You're a braver man than I."

"I daresay you'll find that disciplining your wife is quite a different matter than your sister." The gleam in Edwin's eye made it clear exactly what he meant by that and Hugh gave a small shudder.

"Just remember your wife *is* my sister and I don't want to hear any details."

They both laughed, but there wasn't any real vehemence in Hugh's voice. After all, he'd had occasion to discipline Eleanor when she'd been living beneath her father's roof, as it was good practice for once he was running his own household. But there was no denying that family feeling would make it a very different exercise than Edwin enjoyed with her.

"Besides," said Hugh amiably, "I sincerely doubt Miss Chandler will ever require anything in the way of correction. She's practically a paragon of good behavior."

"And how goes your own courtship?" asked Edwin curiously. "Will you be joining me in matrimonial bliss shortly?"

Snorting, Hugh took a sip of his brandy. "The idea that being married to Eleanor would produce matrimonial bliss..." He shook his head wonderingly as Edwin grinned and raised his own glass in a salute before taking a drink. "But yes, I believe we've come to an arrangement which suits everyone. The announcement should be in the paper this weekend and the date is set for two months from now."

"I have to admit, I'm rather glad I didn't have to wait, although I know Eleanor would have liked a big wedding."

"Eleanor would like a lot of things," said Hugh, shaking his head and grinning. "It wouldn't be good for her to get everything she likes."

"And Miss Chandler? Is she going to get everything she likes?"

Those little stars flitted into Hugh's eyes again and Edwin hid his grin. Doubtless Hugh had been up writing abysmal poetry to Miss Chandlers' eyes again. Fortunately for Miss Chandler, Hugh never shared his creative efforts. Edwin and Wesley had happened upon some written for previous ladies and had teased Hugh so relentlessly that he'd never cared to share any again.

"She'll be well taken care of. In fact, I can't wait to start taking care of her. I'm looking forward to the end of the Season where we can retire to the country and rusticate."

"Sounds boring." Edwin quite preferred the bustle of town life, something he and Hugh had never managed to agree on. Still, despite his preference, Edwin would visit the country quite often since both his parents and Hugh were out there.

"From our talks I gather she's a country girl at heart, enjoys spending time outdoors walking and sketching," said Hugh, ignoring Edwin. "She paints water colors."

"Don't they all."

The men laughed. It was true that every second debutante seemed to claim the activity as an accomplishment. Edwin was intrigued Miss Chandler enjoyed the outdoors though, he had seen her the past few Seasons and she had always seemed to enjoy the balls and glitter of London Society. Then again perhaps such entertainments paled after a few years. A woman who enjoyed the country would be a boon to Hugh; while not quite as anti-social as Edwin's parents, much preferred spending time in the country, especially if he was looking after his horses.

"Eleanor always enjoyed the country too, as I recall," said Edwin thoughtfully. "I shall have to ensure that we visit the estates after our honeymoon."

"Ah, but Eleanor had gotten tired of the country and wanted some town excitement," countered Hugh. "You hadn't seen as much of her the past few years. She can barely talk about anything but fashion and the latest dress she bought and which dress she's going to buy." He rolled his eyes.

Edwin frowned. Hmm. Had Eleanor talked to him about anything else? Of course, they did spend a fair amount of time engaged in things much more pleasurable than conversation. She did talk about those things of course. But most women did. It certainly didn't bother him the way it apparently bothered her brother.

"So where are you taking her?" asked Hugh.

"I was thinking the Manse first," said Edwin thoughtfully. The Manse was where he ran his own estates from, separate from those run by his father the Earl of Clarendon. Speaking of, he should really take Eleanor by to visit his mother and father. He'd already gotten a note from his mother scolding him for not giving them proper notice of his wedding. Not that they would have come into town anyway, his father never came to London if he could help it. Edwin had taken over responsibility for everything needing to be handled in the city as soon as he'd turned eighteen, his father claiming it was for his training to be the Earl. Which is partly why he had so much work to do if he was going to be able to get away with his bride in a few weeks.

"No, no, on your honeymoon," corrected Hugh with a laugh.

"Oh, I was thinking she might enjoy France. The best fashions come from France, so she should like that," he said. Then his mood darkened a little as he remembered the ridiculous sum he'd paid for Eleanor's new wardrobe last week. Maybe not France. He certainly didn't feel like buying her anything more to add to the pile of new dresses. Not that he'd seen one yet, they were still being constructed he supposed.

His hand itched to spank her all over again.

EDWIN'S HAND continued to itch the night of the dinner party. In fact it burned. His wife was wearing one of her new dresses and she'd been clever enough not to show herself until the first of the guests were arriving, at which point she came rushing in all apologetic. Of course, he would not have minded her tardiness under normal circumstances, as this was her first time hostessing even a small dinner party, and she'd been very busy all day with the last-minute preparations, but he could tell from the faint hint of defiance in her expression that she had done so on purpose so he could not force her to go upstairs and change.

The dress was a rich ruby red that looked quite nice with her rosy complexion and honey blonde hair, even if it didn't do anything to bring out her eyes, but it was scandalously low-cut without even a lace fichu to provide some modesty. The dramatic lines of the dress made it cling to her curves, showing far more of her figure than any decent woman should, married or not. It was the kind of dress he would love to see her wear in private, just for him, so he could peel it off of her slowly, after kissing every inch of delicious skin that it revealed. Instead she was wearing it for her first evening as a hostess.

Not only was he furious at her indecency he felt rather humiliated as well. Fortunately the dinner party was so small none of the biggest gossips were invited to see his bride's sartorial mistake. Tongues would still wag, but the knowledge would be second or third hand for the most part. There was nothing he could do but smile grimly at his arriving guests and greet them, pretending his wife didn't look more like a ladybird than a proper Countess. Lord Harrington gave him a sharp look, but the small nod he gave to Edwin indicated he under-stood the younger man's position. Indeed, there was almost a glint of relief in his eyes that Eleanor was now Edwin's problem to deal with and not his. The look he gave his daughter still made her squirm however.

Her brother was not quite so circumspect.

"Good gads, Nell, what are you wearing?" he gasped. Fortunately there was a lull in arrivals and no one overheard his comment, he'd managed to force his voice down to a whisper despite his shock, his face heating with the same embarrassment and outrage Edwin was feeling. "You look like a bleeding light skirt!"

Eleanor gasped in indignation, drawing herself upwards, which had the unfortunate effect of causing her breasts to swell upwards and Edwin had to restrain himself from whipping off his jacket and covering her right then and there.

"Don't *do* that," Hugh hissed at her, his eyes darting wildly around. "You're about to pop out of that dress. I can't believe you wore it."

"You sound like a nagging old prune," Eleanor hissed back at him. "I never took you for a stuffed shirt."

"I never took you for a—"

"Hugh," Edwin's voice interrupted them, calmly, firmly. The siblings both straightened, they hadn't even realized they'd leaned forward for their hissing conversation. "My wife and I will be discussing it later."

The expression on Hugh's face said he hadn't been expecting reproach from his friend. For a moment Eleanor almost felt something like triumph over her brother and gratitude at Edwin for stepping in, but then the import of his words struck her. He wasn't defending her right to wear whatever kind of dress she wanted, he was asserting his right to rebuke her for it. Clenching her tiny fists into her skirts she decided to ignore both of them, turning her head away and pasting a smile on her face as another pair of guests arrived —her friend Grace Greville on the arm of one of the *ton's* most notorious rakes, Lord Conyngham. Scandal itself, considering Grace had not given her husband, Lord Brooke, an heir before taking a lover. He had lovers as well, but the *ton* whispered about Lady Grace because she had not done her duty.

Eleanor didn't care. Grace's mother was a good friend of Eleanor's mother and so the two girls had often been thrown together when they were younger, resulting in a firm friendship. They had not been able to keep up the acquaintance as much after Grace had been married to Lord Brooke during her first Season, but now Eleanor was also married they would be able to spend more time together. It suddenly occurred to her that if she were to live apart from her husband without first providing him with an heir she would garner much of the same reproach Grace had. But Grace was still invited to most of the events during the Season, except by the highest steppers of the *ton*, and surely Eleanor would be as well. Especially since she had no intention of taking lovers.

As they approached Hugh nodded his head at Edwin and disappeared into the drawing room where the other guests were gathered. Soon she and Edwin would join them, Grace and Lord Conyngham were the last to arrive.

Because Grace was her friend, Eleanor made the introductions, trying to ignore the way Conyngham's eyes lingered over her bosom. Under his predatory gaze she felt distinctly undressed and not at all comfortable. No one else had eyed her in such a way, although she quite suddenly realized no one else would have dared. They were all either close friends of Edwin's or married to one of her close friends or one of their family members. If this had been a larger dinner party or a ball there would have been more than Conyngham's eyes roving over her assets. Beside her Edwin seemed to stiffen even more, if that was possible. Too much to hope he hadn't noticed the way Conyngham was looking at her.

So had Grace unfortunately.

"My Eleanor... that is quite a dress," the other lady said. With her raven's wing hair and bright blue eyes, Grace had been considered a Diamond of the First Water upon her debut, and she looked quite splendid in blue silk with a silvery overlay. She also had a higher neckline than Eleanor did. Previously Eleanor had always envied those ladies with those necklines, thinking they must be considered the most beautiful, the most desirable ladies. Now, seeing the way her husband was eying Grace with approval and feeling distinctly uncomfortable with the attention she seemed to have garnered from Conyngham, she was starting to think perhaps her father had had a point about more demure necklines. Grace smiled brilliantly up at Edwin, making Eleanor bristle a little. "I'm sure Lord Villiers quite appreciates its... charms."

The tone of her voice said what her words glossed over—in effect that she was dressed like a tart. Coming from Grace, who was currently one of the most scandalous ladies amongst the *ton*, Eleanor felt that was a little much. She had forgotten how sharp Grace could be. It's not as if Eleanor was trying to poach Conyngham after all, she certainly didn't appreciate him looking at her like she was a dessert he would very much like to nibble.

"I appreciate all of Eleanor's charms," said Edwin, his voice quiet but entirely sincere. "And she has very many."

Grace blinked a little, sensing the light rebuke beneath his words, before putting on her most charming smile and commenting that she'd heard Lady Lucas, another of their friends, was also attending the dinner tonight. The conversation shifted as Eleanor and Edwin led the way to the drawing room, her hand securely on her husband's arm. Somehow the dress she'd been so excited about purchasing and wearing felt like a dismal failure. Next to Grace's elegant beauty she felt tawdry and disenchanted. It was a disheartening experience to feel like a tart when standing next to a woman who was being so brazenly unfaithful to her husband. Not that there was anything unusual about unfaithful marriages in their social class (other than Lord Brooke's lack of heir), but Eleanor had also just come to the startling realization that she couldn't imagine sharing intimacies with anyone but Edwin.

Perhaps such intimacies weren't truly meant for her in that case. There were plenty of women who lived without a husband or lover and had perfectly happy lives. Flitting her glance around their table, Eleanor wondered how many of the couples seated there had happy marriages. She knew her mother was utterly in love with her father, but she discounted that particular marriage because she had no idea how her father felt about her mother other than he used her mother's love to dictate exactly how their household would be run and how her mother would live her life. The other couples... Miss Chandler's parents eyed each other with barely concealed disdain, Grace had her rake and her husband was probably off somewhere with his mistress, her friend Lady Patience had her husband Lord Roger Moore firmly under her thumb although he also had a mistress... and Edwin's other acquaintances were still bachelors. She'd made up for their uneven numbers by inviting her friend Miss Matilda Brething who had come with her mother. Mr. Brething was out of town. Probably with his mistress as well.

The entire situation made Eleanor feel rather miserable as she faced the fact that she didn't particularly like the idea of Edwin having a mistress. And yet unless she was willing to perform her wifely duties he would certainly go looking for one. Even if she did perform her wifely duties, he might still go looking for one. For all she knew he already had one.

No... she thought, studying him opposite her at the table. No, she didn't think he would be the type to still have a mistress so near to his wedding, not at the beginning of the marriage. Besides, when would he have the time? He was either working or in her bed, making her forget why she wanted, needed, to get away.

The best thing she could do was keep on with her plan. Obviously her emotions were becoming far too entangled. Any more of this and she'd end up like her mother, so in love she'd do whatever her husband said and forgive anything he did. Did her father have a mistress? If so, he was very discreet. The other women around the table might not have the happiest marriages, but they were happy in other parts of their lives. From what Eleanor could see, love only made a person weak and she was determined to be strong.

Besides, after tonight she doubted her husband would want anything to do with her anyway.

Pasting a brilliant smile on her face, she started up a conversation with Lord Moore, who was seated to her right. Her father was on her left but he was already speaking in earnest with Mrs. Brething about Mr. Brething's horses. As the first course was brought in she kept her eye on Edwin, wondering when he'd realize what she'd done.

CHAPTER 6

*E*dwin was going to kill his wife. Slowly. Painfully.

Their party was four courses into dinner and he was starving.

He remembered with clarity the exact moment of his downfall, last week when she'd suddenly started acting amenable after a long conversation about his favorite dishes and those he disliked. There was an astonishing lack of any of the former and a superfluity of the latter. Even those dishes he did enjoy, such as a good fish, had been rendered inedible to him by the mustard sauce. He hated mustard. She must have directed the chef to slather it on.

Mostly he'd pushed his food around on his plate, forced himself to take a few bites for politeness sake (and also because he was so hungry even creamed turnips were starting to look appealing) and concentrated on entertaining his guests. Also on trying to keep the furious glitter from his eyes. He could see Eleanor watching him out of the corner of his eye, but he refused to look at her. If he did he wouldn't be able to hide how furious he was with her.

Instead he concentrated on getting to know Miss Chandler better, a task made more difficult by the fact that it was becoming increasingly obvious she and Eleanor's friend Lady Grace were acquainted and they did *not* enjoy each other's company. Personally, he didn't particularly enjoy Lady Grace's company either, but he hadn't made the seating arrangements so he was stuck with her for now. The sly barbs she'd tried to stick into Eleanor at the beginning of the evening had seemed to be just momentary female jealousy over the fact her escort had been eying Eleanor's charms—which hadn't made him pleased with Conyngham either, and even less pleased with Eleanor for giving him the opportunity.

It was obvious Grace was used to having male attention focused on her although surely she'd shared with Eleanor in the past. The two of them set each other off beautifully with Grace's midnight hair against the sunlight golden strands of Eleanor's, the startlingly pale sky blue of Grace's eyes that looked almost violet to Eleanor's brighter sapphires. But Grace didn't seem to have the inner sweetness under the hard outer shell he knew Eleanor possessed. While Eleanor might play at being a pampered spoiled brat there was much more to her beneath that. Grace was all crystalline hard edges and corrupted power... would this be what Eleanor could have become after a season of being labeled a Diamond of the First Water, with countless men falling at her feet and fighting to win her hand? Edwin was fervently grateful he'd married Nell before she could become jaded and he had no intention of allowing her to do so now.

"Miss Chandler, I've been meaning to wish you happy on your engagement to the Viscount," Lady Grace said, but even the smile she graced upon Miss Chandler seemed to have a hard edge. Miss Chandler gripped her fork unnecessarily hard, Edwin noted, but showed no other reaction. "It must be such a relief to you and your family."

The slight paling of Miss Chandler's face made Edwin want to step in and save her but he couldn't help but feel it was Hugh's duty to protect his future bride from the sly reminder of the Chandler's financial situation. Unfortunately, Hugh's attention was being taken up by Mrs. Chandler, who seemed to feel it her duty to keep her future son-in-law conversationally entertained. Going by the look on Hugh's face he probably would have preferred it if she hadn't.

"Thank you, Lady Brooke," said Miss Chandler. Although her looks weren't to Edwin's taste, he had to admit she had the most amazing emerald eyes, right now they looked hard as diamonds as she tilted her head upwards to meet Lady Grace's gaze. "I appreciate hearing it from you personally, although Al—Lord Brooke had already wished us happy on behalf of you both."

Conyngham choked on his wine and Lady Grace looked like she might actually leap across the table at Miss Chandler. Mentioning Grace's husband was almost guaranteed to send her flying across the handle. And had Miss Chandler almost referred to him by his Christian name? If so, it must mean she knew him well, was perhaps even close friends. Brooke's lands were near to her family's estate after all. Why on earth had Eleanor seated these two anywhere near each other? Unless she didn't know... it was possible the guilty look on her face was just for starving him, not for both starving him and giving him miserable company. There were undercurrents between these two women which threatened to disrupt the entire dinner party if he didn't do something to stop them now.

"And I'm pleased to welcome you to the family," he said cheerfully, cutting the tension as best he could with false brevity. "Not just because Eleanor's my wife. Hugh and I have been like brothers for years. Has he told you about the time we tried to make a pig's bladder explode in his tutor's closet?"

"No," said Miss Chandler, turning her wide green eyes to him. There wasn't any real interest in her face, but that hadn't been the point anyway.

"Edwin, don't you dare or I'll tell her about the time you tried to convince Eleanor the house was haunted," Hugh threatened. As Edwin had expected, the mere mention of the bladder incident had garnered Hugh's attention away from Mrs. Chandler and back to paying proper attention to Miss Chandler, which meant Edwin could get back to focusing on ways to kill his wife.

With a little wave, he summoned one of the footmen over.

"What's the next course?"

"Beef rubbed with pepper and mustard seeds—"

Edwin shook his head, cutting the man off and sending him back to his place. His wife was going to have a red hot bottom to match her dress tonight.

～

ALTHOUGH SHE DID her best to avoid her husband, Eleanor didn't move quite quickly enough as the women headed to the drawing room to leave the men to retreat to the library and their cigars and port. She let out a little squeak as her husband gripped her upper arm, pulling her into one of the hallway alcoves as the rest of the ladies tittered and chattered their way to the other room.

"I'm sorry," she said immediately, gasping for air as the shock of how quickly he'd caught her reverberated through her. The words came automatically as she realized she was a bit frightened; no matter how angry he might be it wasn't like Edwin to ignore the rules of proper behavior, not with an audience. Had she pushed him farther than she'd meant to?

"If you're not now, you will be later," he said a little grimly. "But that's not why I'm here."

"It's not?" she asked, relaxing a little bit, but then she looked up into his hooded dark eyes and realized she shouldn't have relaxed at all. All signs said *danger*. There was no heat in Edwin's eyes, not of passion or anger, just icy coldness that seemed to slice right through her to the bone. Never before had she seen him look at her like that, as if she was a stranger.

"What's going on between Lady Grace and Miss Chandler?"

"Going on?" she echoed. For a moment the heat of anger flared in Edwin's eyes and she realized it sounded like she was prevaricating. Shaking her head she tried to think. "I don't know, I didn't even know they were acquainted. Are you sure there's something going on?"

The tight hold his fingers had around her arm relaxed a little bit as he studied her face, seeing the honesty. Of course, Eleanor could lie when she needed to, but he'd taken her by such surprise her expression was completely open.

"There's definitely something going on," he said, his voice still rather grim. "Keep them away from each other. And we *will* be having a discussion about this evening's dinner later tonight."

Then he let her go. Shaken but knowing she needed to attend to her guests, Eleanor hurried away to the drawing room where she found Grace had seated herself on the settee speaking with Eleanor's mother and Mrs. and Miss Brething, while Mrs. and Miss Chandler were conversing closer to the fireplace with Lady Moore. Wondering what Edwin had thought was the problem, Eleanor went to join Lady Grace's circle first.

The idle chatter about the latest fashion plates should have taken up most of her attention, normally she adored talking fashion—especially with Grace who always looked absolutely divine, but the conversation just reminded her of the dress she was currently wearing. Indeed, as the discussion continued she became more and more aware of her mother's and Mrs. Brething's disapproving glances at her neckline, accompanied by her daughter's wide-eyed occasional stares and blushes. Eleanor was quite sure the young woman was picturing herself in a similar dress. Color rose in Eleanor's cheeks as she decided she'd entertained these ladies long enough and quietly slipped away to join the other circle, holding her head high.

Lady Moore was holding forth about her husband's latest horse purchase, which seemed to interest Mrs. Chandler quite a bit and Miss Chandler not at all. Yet Miss Chandler seemed perfectly content to sit and listen to the older matron's conversation rather than joining the other circle and discussing fashion. Perhaps there *was* something going on between Miss Chandler and Lady Grace, Eleanor couldn't imagine any other reason Miss Chandler would still be sitting here.

"So we're to be sisters," she said brightly, after exchanging the usual pleasantries. The two older ladies had quickly delved back into their conversation, allowing Eleanor the opportunity to speak a little aside to Miss Chandler. "Have you started planning the wedding yet?"

"Oh yes, thank you for asking, Lady Hyde." said Miss Chandler rather shyly. "My mother speaks of nothing else these days."

"Please, call me Eleanor," she said impulsively reaching out and taking Miss Chandler's hand. "There's no need to stand on ceremony when we're going to be sisters soon."

"Then you must call me Irene," said Miss Chandler, but Eleanor didn't miss the way Irene's eyes slid over to Grace for a moment before returning to Eleanor. Was she worried Grace had said something about her? "I always wanted a sister closer to my age."

"Hugh mentioned you have younger sisters, but he didn't say how old they were."

"Rosalie is fourteen and Miranda is twelve. My brother Alfred is sixteen and I was always rather disappointed he wasn't a girl."

Both of them giggled.

"I always wanted a sister, period," confessed Eleanor. "I thought Hugh was rather useless, it never occurred to me until recently that he could provide me with the sister my parents hadn't."

"Ah yes," said Irene, although the light in her green eyes dimmed a little. Her smile seemed just a tad less bright and Eleanor couldn't help but wonder why. "But your new husband does not have any sisters?"

"No, he's an only child. I think that's why he became so attached to Hugh and their friend Wesley. The three of them are more like brothers than anything else. I used to think he only saw me as an annoying little sister but..." Eleanor's voice trailed off as she blushed, realizing her thoughts and conversation had almost turned to a place not entirely appropriate.

"So you're a love match?" asked Irene, her voice a little skeptical.

"No." Giving a little cough Eleanor tried to blunt the sharpness in her voice, pasting a false social smile on her face. "No ah... we're just, we've known each other for so long. We're... companions, I suppose you could say. We've known each other for so long that we do care for one another of course." She gave a light little laugh that felt and sounded rather hollow.

Irene nodded as if Eleanor had confirmed something she'd already known. "That's the most one can expect I suppose." She leaned into Eleanor conspiratorially. "Can I tell you a secret? And you won't tell anyone, not even Hugh?"

GOLDEN ANGEL

"Of course," Eleanor said, leaning in.

"And not Lady Brooke, please," said Irene, her eyes sliding back over to the other circle of females.

"Is there something between the two of you? Edwin had mentioned it might be best if the two of you weren't seated as closely as you had been at dinner."

"We don't get along," said Irene firmly.

Eleanor nodded. "She is one of my dearest friends, but I know she does not get along with everyone. Still, dear friend or not, you may trust me because I am sure we are going to become the best of friends and soon we're going to be sisters. I will not betray your confidence."

"Thank you," Irene reached out and gave Eleanor's hand a small press, her voice lowering even further as the two young ladies leaned close to each other. Not that the matrons seated with them were paying attention to their conversation but it was obvious Irene didn't want to risk anyone overhearing the slightest word. "I used to hope for a love match but from my observations they happen rarely, if at all. I think companionship or friendship is the best one can hope for in a marriage. Do you think Hugh will be content with that?"

Now Eleanor hesitated. She knew very well Hugh was already more than a bit smitten with his bride to be, on the other hand smitten didn't exactly denote *love*. Perhaps he could be content with a wife who wanted nothing more than companionship or friendship? But then what if he wanted something passionate, something intense, something... something like what she and Edwin had? Or what if he wanted an adoring wife like their mother?

Unfortunately, before she could think of how to answer Irene, the drawing room door opened to admit Banks with the tea and the men following behind. Edwin entered in the middle of the pack, immediately drawing her eye. He looked every inch the handsome gentleman in his claret waistcoat and evening dress, a small smile on his face as he scanned the room. Seeing Eleanor seated with Miss Chandler, and Lady Grace on the other side of the room, he gave his wife a small nod of approval, which for some reason only grated on her.

The whole point of this evening, after all, was to make him angry and force him to realize his disciplinary tactics weren't working. She wasn't supposed to be doing things to get his approval, but at the same time she realized part of her wanted to. Which just frightened her even more. Was she already turning into her mother after only a few weeks of marriage? Did this mean she loved him?

It couldn't. Surely she'd know immediately if she'd fallen in love. The tingling feeling just underneath her skin was just a symptom of the sensual desires he'd awoken in her, the ones he fed every night. Perhaps part of her was reluctant to give up the pleasures of the bedroom, but that wasn't enough for her to cease in her efforts to gain control over her life and marriage.

Before tonight Edwin hadn't always appreciated the time after dinner when the men and women would separate. Often he'd been more interested in talking to the ladies but this evening it had been almost necessary to his equilibrium to have time away from Eleanor. And also to discreetly send Banks to get him a sandwich so he wasn't quite so starving. A glass of port and a cigar, some friendly banter with the gentlemen, and he was feeling much less murderous.

Not that Eleanor wasn't going to pay for her transgressions. In fact, he'd realized the many antics of this evening called for a much harsher punishment then he'd ever given her before, but he was now going to be able to approach her discipline from a place of tranquility rather than anger. He certainly never wanted to be anything but calm and disciplined himself when he was punishing her.

Following Hugh, who veered straight for Irene, Edwin sat next to his wife and spent the rest of the evening doing the pretty from Eleanor's side. He didn't allow her to move more than a foot away from him once all evening, which obviously only increased her anxiety and trepidation. The more he smiled, the more jittery she became.

Finally, they were able to sweep their guests out the door, the small party a success as far as all of them were concerned. Lady Grace and Miss Chandler had managed to stay separated for the entirety of the evening following dinner, which made for a much more amiable gathering overall and Hugh had been quite happy to dance attendance on his soon-to-be bride while Conyngham had kept Lady Grace quite distracted.

"I'm going to go speak with Mrs. Hester," said Eleanor as soon as her parents had said their farewell and left. "I'd like to have her opinion on the evening, what she thought worked well and what we might improve upon next time."

While Edwin was sure that was true, and he was pleased to know Eleanor was assuming her duties in regards to being his hostess, he also knew she was trying to avoid being alone with him. Obviously she was aware of the trouble she was in.

"You may speak with her tomorrow," he said firmly, grasping her by the elbow with a firm hand. He looked at Banks. "Tell the staff we are done for the evening and we should not be disturbed for the rest of the night."

"Very good, my lord," said Banks with a little bow-like movement as Eleanor let out a small whimper.

The expression on her face flitted back and forth between fear and a kind of determination, making Edwin wonder exactly what she had been thinking by serving all food he disliked if she was so anxious about being disciplined. Sometimes he wondered if women's minds worked anything at all like men's; living with Eleanor he was beginning to come to the conclusion they didn't. If she didn't want to be punished, why had she gone out of the way to do something she knew she'd be punished for? Not only had her menu been malicious, but the inappropriate dress she was wearing was another point of defiance. She could have made it more modest with a fichu but instead she'd chosen to flaunt herself before their family and friends. He still got a flash of jealous anger whenever he thought about Conyngham eying the creamy swells of her breasts, despite the fact the man had done nothing more than look at what Eleanor was offering.

As Edwin pulled her along towards their bedroom Eleanor remembered she was trying to show him she wouldn't be cowed by his discipline, that no matter what he did she would keep doing what she wanted to.

Unfortunately that determination was somewhat undermined by

the fact she felt rather guilty about how little he'd truly been able to eat during dinner. She'd seen him manfully forcing himself to taste some of the dishes. Only someone who knew him well, who had studied his face while he'd eaten dishes he'd enjoyed, would have noticed the tightness around his mouth and eyes, the slight grimaces. Although she'd done her best to pretend she wasn't watching him she hadn't been able to keep herself from sneaky little glances. It wasn't in her nature to be intentionally malicious, especially when she wasn't truly angry with Edwin, and so she rather felt as though she deserved some kind of punishment for that mean trick. The guilt which had quietly been growing all night now felt fit to bursting.

So it was with mixed feelings that she entered their bedroom, half-defiant and half-guilty. Edwin didn't seem angry anymore, although she knew he'd been enraged by the end of dinner. Either he had better control over his facial expressions than she thought or he had calmed down. However she knew calm didn't equate to forgiving.

Turning to face her husband Eleanor's body language was a study in contradictions. Her chin was high and her hands were fisted at her sides, but her shoulders were hunched and her eyes were wary, her face flushing and paling by degrees. Alone, standing in front of him, she couldn't help but notice how attractive he looked, despite the blank expression on his face. Part of her fervently wished she hadn't deliberately ruined this evening; she was quite certain if she had behaved then they'd be finding wondrous, glorious pleasure together, the way they did almost every night. At least if she'd just worn the dress then she wouldn't have merited more than a spanking.

Looking at her husband's forbidding countenance she was sure her punishment was going to be much more severe.

"Take off your dress," he said in a short, clipped voice, before turning away from her to go into his dressing room.

With trembling fingers Eleanor did the best she could, but she couldn't reach all the buttons in the back. When Edwin returned he was wearing only his breeches and shirt, his hand wrapped around a birch rod. She felt her knees weaken and her mouth dry as she stared at the slender branches, tied with a pretty blue ribbon. The color matched her eyes exactly.

"Please, Edwin, no," she begged, unable to take her eyes off of the disciplinary instrument.

"Turn around," he ordered. Closing her eyes, the defiance leaking out of her, Eleanor did as he commanded. She could feel his fingers moving against her, undoing the last buttons of her dress. He helped her shrug it off and then he threw it to the side of them with a violent movement. With his help it only took a few more minutes before she stood completely bare and vulnerable.

"Pretty Eleanor," Edwin murmured, putting his fingers under her chin and tipping her head up to look at him. She let tears fill her big blue eyes as she pressed her hands against his chest, staring pleadingly into his dark ones which were as hard as stone. "Pretty wife. Why are you so naughty?"

She bit into her plump lower lip. Because this wasn't the marriage she wanted. Because she was slowly losing control, not just of her life but of her emotions. Because if she didn't make herself hate him, she might start to do more than care for him. She might start to *love* him. Then she would be just like her mother, bending to the will of a dictatorial husband who didn't have a care for what she might want. Even if Edwin cared for her she couldn't imagine him giving up any power in a relationship; he would use her love, the way her father used her mother's, to arrange the life *he* wanted.

So she had to be bad, bad enough he would realize his disciplinary measures did not work on her, bad enough he would let her go away and stay with friends or family, live the life she wanted.

Edwin watched a strange array of expressions flicker over his wife's pretty face, too quickly for him to interpret any of them. He truly did want to know why she'd gone out of her way to make tonight miserable for him, it wasn't something he would have ever expected of her. That kind of antagonizing stunt wasn't in Eleanor's usual personality. It had been a calculated ploy but for what benefit? She had to know she would be punished.

"Are you going to apologize?" he asked. Not that it would stop him from disciplining her. She deserved it, nay needed it. Hugh had been right, let her get away with little things and she would run with the freedom. Eleanor needed constancy, she needed to know where the line was and she would always be disciplined for crossing it—or in this case for playing complete havoc with it. But if she apologized he would go a little lighter on her. Just a little.

But the obstinate creature shook her head, her teeth releasing her lip as her chin jutted forward. "I know of no need to apologize."

"Really?" He took a deep breath and raised his eyes to stare at the ceiling for a moment in exasperation. "Unacceptable Eleanor. Even for a prevarication I expected better from you." Especially since it was quite clear to both of them that she knew exactly what she needed to apologize for, now she was just being obstinate.

CHAPTER 7

The tension Eleanor was feeling was almost overwhelming. She didn't know what to do; she owed Edwin an apology because truly her behavior had been rather abominable when it came to the dinner menu she'd planned. But she also felt like she should continue her defiance, show him she wasn't just going to give in because he'd brought out a birch. No matter what kind of punishment, spanking, birching, she couldn't give up if she was going to convince him it would be less trouble to just let her go her own way.

Which meant she was going to have to take the birching and then keep up her behavior. Not a pleasant prospect but surely that would show him he should be the one to give up. Maybe if she brought it up now he would give in.

"Why should I apologize for creating a dinner all of our guests and I enjoyed?" she asked haughtily, trying to stifle the vestiges of her guilt. It was hard to be haughty when she was completely nude and Edwin was not, but she did her best. Crossing her arms under her breasts she lifted her chin, pretending she didn't notice and didn't care about her lack of clothing. "If you don't like the way I plan a menu then perhaps we shouldn't share meals. Or a house."

Edwin stiffened. Where had this come from? He'd rather thought he and Eleanor were doing quite well together, other than her apathy when it came to taking any responsibility towards running the household. But he thought their relationship had been growing, that she was actually beginning to feel some affection for him as he felt for her, despite the circumstances of their marriage. She certainly hadn't had any reluctance about sharing his bed every night once he got her there, although she admittedly required some coaxing, but he'd thought that had been a show of maidenly virtue. Which was quickly shed, once her passion was aroused.

"Is there something about our marriage which leaves you unsatisfied?" he asked softly, his voice almost a warning. Since deciding upon Eleanor for his wife he had known he would not take a mistress; he saw it as disrespectful towards her and he certainly wouldn't countenance her taking a lover, no matter how discreet. Was that what tonight's dress had been about? Did she want a house of her own so she could meet a lover there?

"Not unsatisfied," she said slowly. The flash of hurt she'd seen on Edwin's face had surprised her, but she didn't want to add to it. "But this is not the kind of marriage I had imagined. I don't think I should get a birching just for planning a menu you didn't like."

Something tense inside of Edwin relaxed. Just more manipulations. That he could handle. He wasn't as surprised now. Eleanor had wanted her way when it came to getting married, which he had some sympathy for, and now she was lashing out because she hadn't gotten what she wanted. Still, he couldn't let her behavior go unacknowledged, especially since she'd piled insult onto injury tonight. He'd obviously been too lenient with her, curious as to what she was planning; that ended now.

"You aren't getting a birching because you planned a menu I didn't like, you're getting a birching for deliberately disrespecting me by purposefully choosing each dish to ensure it was something I wouldn't enjoy eating. You did it willfully and maliciously after having an entire conversation with me about my eating preferences. I realize this might not be the marriage you would have chosen for yourself, but instead of trying to work on our relationship—which I think

89

could be quite enjoyable for both of us with very little effort—you are wallowing in self-pity and doing your best to sabotage it." Eleanor's jaw worked, but no sound came from her mouth. The expression on her face showed both guilt and a stubbornness to hold to her position. "From now on things are going to change. You have had plenty of time to accustom yourself to being married and I have tolerated your behavior for long enough. There will be no more handing your responsibilities to Mrs. Hester to take care of, you will behave yourself with propriety and you will dress as behooves your station. When you do not, you will be punished."

"That's not fair!" She pouted her lower lip at him, although it was almost ludicrous looking as she was obviously more furious than upset. It was hard to look like a victim when every inch of her body screamed her desire to wring his neck. "I'm a grown woman and I should be able to choose what I do with my days and my wardrobe."

"It's more than fair and you know it." Grimly, Edwin gestured with his hand, twirling it and indicating she should turn about. The hot flush of anger on his wife's cheeks, the glittering sparkle in her bright blue eyes and the sight of her naked body was having its usual effect on him. He was going to enjoy giving her bottom a well-deserved thrashing and then indulging in their usual evening's pleasures. "Turn around and bend over the bed Eleanor, or I will tie you in place and your punishment will be much worse."

Looking at the determination on her husband's face, Eleanor knew he was speaking nothing but the unadulterated truth. Now her lower lip truly did tremble as she finally realized she may have pushed him too far, although even now he wasn't reacting from anger. She'd expected a spanking, but nothing more than that. And he would tie in her place?

It suddenly occurred to Eleanor that perhaps she'd misjudged Edwin; the hard look on his face made it clear he was more than willing to follow through with his threat. This was certainly more than she'd bargained for. Yet she was no longer the same young woman who had acceded to the punishments her father deemed necessary and Edwin certainly treated her differently in other regards. Perhaps she could convince him towards leniency or even distract him entirely.

"Please Edwin, I am sorry," she said, putting the small amount of guilt she actually did feel into her voice to convince him of her sincerity. Looking up at him pleadingly, she stepped forward, her hands dropping to her sides and revealing her body, hoping to distract him with her nudity. She'd had plenty of time to learn how appealing she was, physically, to him. "Truly, I am, it was malicious and wrong and I wasn't really thinking." Placing her hands on his chest she peered up at him through lowered lashes, feeling triumphant as she felt his body shift under her hands, saw the flash of arousal as he looked down at her.

"Apology accepted," he said, his voice tight as he controlled his impulse to forgo the punishment, throw his wife down on his bed and ravish her senseless. It seemed Eleanor had found a new way to be manipulative; it hadn't taken her long to go from innocent to seductress apparently. In other circumstances he would have been quite pleased to have her approaching him this way. "Now turn around and go bend over the bed."

"But Edwin!" she protested, shock writ clear across her face that he wasn't taking what she was offering.

"Just because you have found it in yourself to admit you did something wrong doesn't mean you won't have to reap the consequences for it," he said sternly. It was so close to something her father had said to her before that Eleanor gaped at him, unable to think of a single rebuttal. "Tempting me with your delightful body just shows you are still trying to manipulate the situation, rather than showing any true remorse. If you want to convince me you truly regret your actions then you will do as I say and take your punishment like a good wife."

Now she was truly torn. Eleanor didn't want to be a good wife because if she pleased Edwin then he would be less agreeable to living apart from her. Already he'd shown himself to oppose such an arrangement and she knew she hadn't been a very good wife at all. Yet she also didn't want more of a punishment than she'd already earned.

Deciding there was no point in antagonizing him further at present, which would only increase this punishment, she slowly turned and walked towards the bed with her head down to show her contriteness. Truly, however, she was contrite she'd thought Edwin would be this easy to handle. There would be no quick agreement from him, this contest of wills was going to be a long and drawn out affair. She would have to prove over and over again that she would not be managed by him or deterred by his discipline before he would accept she would not be the wife he wanted and would allow her to go her own way. Obviously the idea of living separately did not yet appeal to him. It would be easier for her to do so if she avoided incurring any particularly large punishments.

The sight of his wife—*finally*—moving obediently to take her punishment had an effect on Edwin like he'd never experienced before. It wasn't that he wanted to punish Eleanor, at least not to the level he felt was needful for today's transgressions, but he didn't think any man would be unaffected by the vision Eleanor presented. Completely nude, bent over the bed and braced on her forearms, her hair still in its elaborate coiffure so that the long line of her back was displayed, and the creamy swell of her buttocks being offered up for his pleasure and punishment; the throbbing in his cock was becoming painful as he struggled to control himself.

Although unintended, the wait for Edwin to move towards her was having a rather salutary effect on Eleanor. Tense anticipation wracked her and she heartily wished she'd decided earlier to take the long road, rather than try to rush her goals with the demonstration she'd made with dinner. Or she could have been more subtle. Thrown in a few dishes she had known he liked. But no, she'd been impatient and overconfident, and too impetuously sulky to thoroughly think through the consequences of her actions.

When she finally heard the rustle of clothing as Edwin moved towards her she actually felt relieved. Waiting for her punishment was torturous, especially since she couldn't help but spend the time castigating herself and Eleanor certainly did not like to dwell on her failures. Not that she'd ever had many. She'd even handled her father better than she'd managed Edwin; what was it about the man that threw her mind so badly off center?

A finger stroked down the center of her back, making her shiver—and not with fear or cold.

"Just get it over with," she said waspishly, feeling a little flare of anger that he would try to arouse her at a time like this.

"Very well," he said, sounding rather amused. Eleanor didn't dare look at his face because if he did look amused she wasn't sure she could keep a hold of her temper. Her husband's hand curved over her bottom, squeezing the flesh hard, just on the edge of roughly and she tried to ignore the heat it kindled at her core. "First you're going to get a spanking for that dress—which you knew was inappropriate. If the rest of your new wardrobe is anything like it then you will make the gowns more decent with a fichu."

Biting her lip Eleanor glared at the bed cover beneath her face. Her body was feeling rather conflicted at the moment. The way Edwin was palming her bottom was quite arousing, she felt angry all over again as he dictated how she would dress, and yet she also felt ashamed of the way she'd looked tonight in front of their guests. Despite knowing he was correct she resented that he felt the need to inform her of what she already knew, what she'd already decided. Now it would look like she was doing it to follow his orders and not because she was intelligent enough to realize the dress hadn't had the effect she'd intended.

"I had already decided that anyway," she muttered, unable to keep the words in even though she was sure he wouldn't believe her.

"I'm glad to hear it." There didn't seem to be any insincerity in his voice, but the approval grated on her anyway.

Blast him, she didn't need his approval.

SMACK!

Eleanor gasped and rocked forwards on her arms as Edwin's hand came down hard on her right buttock, followed by a quick cracking spank to her left.

SMACK! SMACK! SMACK! SMACK!

It was as if he'd separated her buttocks into quadrants, his hand coming down on each of them in turn. Lower right, upper right, upper left, lower left.

Digging her fingers into the bedclothes as her bottom began to heat, the hard smacks stinging and burning, Eleanor couldn't stop the small distressed sounds her husband's spanking elicited. His hand was very strong, very firm, and as powerful as a board. Bending over the bed like this was much less intimate than being over his lap, removing the distraction of having his hard body pressed against her.

SMACK! SMACK!

The slaps to the sensitive crease between her thighs and buttocks rocked her forward again and she gave out a little cry, burying her face into the bed sheets. That bloody hurt! And yet...

As Edwin rubbed his wife's buttocks, admiring the pinkish hue they had taken on, he also noticed that beneath those rosy cheeks her womanhood was beginning to dew with wetness. Knowing she couldn't see his face he grinned, thanking whatever saint was responsible for his luck in having Eleanor to wife. Still, she would feel roundly disciplined by the end of this session, of that he was determined. Digging his fingers into her flesh, he almost groaned at the soft sound she made, a cross between pleasure and pain as he further abused her bottom.

Raising his hand again he brought it down hard, his eyes lingering over the darker pink of his prints every time he landed a fresh smack on her flesh.

"OW!" Eleanor thrust her hands back, covering her bottom protectively. "I thought you were done!"

"Not yet, now move your hands Eleanor."

"But I'm *sorry*! I won't wear a dress like that again, I promise!" Despite her words, Edwin noted his wife sounded much more outraged than remorseful. She was mad because she thought he'd stopped and she was willing to say whatever she needed to make that a reality.

"I'm not saying you can't wear it, just not where anyone other than I will see you," he said as he took her hands by her wrists and put them back on either side of her head. As he leaned forward to do so she turned her head just enough to glare at him, making it obvious she currently had no intention of allowing him to enjoy the sight of her in such a revealing garment. Edwin manfully swallowed the laugh which threatened and raised one sardonic eyebrow at her. Flushing, Eleanor turned her face back to the bed and put her hands around it to keep him from being able to see her at all. "Ten more."

His wife made a little sound, which he decided to ignore although he was fairly certain she'd just cursed at him. At least she hadn't done it loudly enough for him to hear, in which case he would have felt obliged to add to the number of slaps her buttocks would receive.

Eleanor struggled not to cry out as Edwin peppered the last flurry of spankings onto her already hot and pain-filled bottom. To her frustration, despite the fact that it *hurt* and was incredibly undigni-fied, not to mention infuriating, one part of her body seemed to enjoy it. Even though she wasn't over his lap she knew she was moist between her legs, her sheath priming itself for him the same way it did when he caressed and kissed her. The strange response was the worst part of the punishment as far as she was concerned, especially because she was sure her husband's all-too-observant eyes couldn't fail to miss the evidence of her arousal.

Once he was done he let her weight drop onto the bed, ignoring the tears already sparking into her eyes. Reaching back she rubbed at the hot, tight skin across her punished globes, trying to soothe the ache. Almost immediately Edwin had her wrists in his hand again.

"Absolutely not, Eleanor," he said in a cold voice. "I know you know better than to rub." It was easy for him to wrap the long fingers of one hand around both of her wrists, holding her arms so they bent at the elbow and her hands were pressed against the small of her back. "Do you need me to hold your hands during the birching?"

"No," she said decisively, shaking her head as if to shake the tears from her eyes. Somehow having Edwin hold her in place so easily only made the situation more humiliating and she knew from the birchings she'd received at her father's hand that she could hold herself in place with nothing more than sheer determination.

For a moment Edwin held onto his wife's tiny wrists, marveling at how slim and bird-like her arms were. Part of him wanted to continue holding her in place, enjoying the domination over her, but if she wanted to try and control herself then he was inclined to let her. Besides, he would have a better view of her luscious bottom if he could step away a bit. The idea of tying her in place was extremely appealing, but he didn't want her to associate bondage with pain, not unless she required it. Reluctantly releasing her, he picked up the swishy birch. The branches were quite whippy and he knew they would sting but not cause any undue damage.

"Spread your legs," he ordered. "And point your toes in."

Remembering the first time he'd seen Eleanor birched, in a position very similar to this, he couldn't stop the throb of heat that went straight to his cock. Perhaps he shouldn't be enjoying her punishment quite as much as he was but Eleanor was an extremely attractive and sensual woman, and even a punishment became an erotic experience with her. The creaminess of her skin around her rosy bottom, the flash of wet pink flesh at the center of her cuntpurse, the swollen lips pouting enticingly from their frame of damp, honey-gold curls. All of it seemed designed to raise a man's ardor, no matter the circumstances. As he raised his arm he wondered if she would be as wet and aroused after her birching as she was after her spankings.

The birch fell across her pink bottom, leaving streaks of darker red as Eleanor let out a gasping cry. Her body bowed backwards a little, her fingers digging into the bed sheets. A second blow fell across her quivering bottom, slightly higher than the first, leaving new dark welts across her flesh, stinging like a thousand angry bees attacking the already sensitized skin of her bottom. With every strike her body jerked, although the birch fell five times before she truly cried out, her muscles flexing as she did her best to hold herself in position.

"I'M SORRY!" she said, her voice muffled by the bed sheets, desperate for the punishment to end, hoping a spontaneous apology might end the lashing across her burning skin. Still, even now, contrite as she was, her pride couldn't quite allow herself to speak clearly or to face her husband. Another stroke fell across her already flaming bottom and she choked back an outraged protest. Eleanor was becoming quite heartily sorry she'd provoked her husband in such a manner; why couldn't she have been more patient? Why did she have to make a production of things? She'd regretted the menu almost as soon as her fantasy had been made into reality, why hadn't she realized before-hand that such a plan would not only result in a disciplining from her husband, but also the uncomfortable guilt?

A blow landed diagonally across the pouting folds of her sex, making Eleanor howl and causing the pouting lips to plump, an angry pink beneath the thatch of golden hairs. The tension in her body seemed to collapse and Eleanor no longer braced herself against the bed but lay across it, submitting to the birch as Edwin delivered the last three blows across her welted and burning red bottom.

By the time he was finished he was breathing heavily, staring at his wife's lusciously tormented flesh as he dropped the birch to the ground beneath him. Kneeling behind her, blood seemed to pound in his ears as he gripped her bottom cheeks in both hands, squeezing the tender cheeks and making her writhe. The heat seemed to sear his palms, the musky humidity of her quim calling to him. Everything about her was hot and squirming, inflaming his loins in a way that savaged his self-control.

"Edwin..." she said in a shaky voice as her husband squeezed her bottom, bringing with it a fresh surge of pain and yet something else too, something tingling along her nerves all the way up her spine and left her feeling breathless.

But surely... surely he couldn't want to do *that* right now.

His HANDS PUSHED at her skin, separating her buttocks and she could feel his hot breath on her open sex. Eleanor cried out a protest, trying to push herself up as Edwin leaned forward and planted his mouth onto her swollen folds, his tongue sliding up the center and wreaking havoc with her senses. Bent over, completely exposed, her bottom throbbed painfully as Edwin began an erotic assault below it, his weight on his hands pressing her hips into the bed and making it impossible for her to escape this new humiliation as her body betrayed her.

"EDWIN, *no*... we can't... you just *punished me*..." Eleanor clawed at the bed sheets, her legs trembling with weakness as his tongue pressed into her. If she had been supporting her own weight she would have fallen as pure pleasure lashed through her with stunning swiftness, mingling with the ache in her buttocks and confusing her utterly. Despite the tears of pain still clinging to her eyelashes, the flames of desire in her core were already igniting, craving the tender tracings of his tongue, the rough abrasion of his hands against her skin.

"And now you're forgiven," he purred from behind her, slipping two fingers into her sopping heat and groaning with lust as she contracted around him. Fascinated by the welts on her bottom he began tracing them with his tongue, feeling the struggle in her flesh as she attempted to throw off the erotic need that had awakened inside of her, trying to grasp her outrage and dignity. Edwin did his best to thwart her efforts, pumping his fingers back and forth in her hot tunnel as he licked and kissed the bruised flesh of her bottom, massaging it with his free hand.

"Nooooooo," Eleanor said, moaning, but it was as much a protest against herself as it was against him. Her husband had long since learned how to snare her senses; she was melting beneath his caresses, his hand gentling as he rubbed her abused rear in an almost comforting manner. The clever fingers inside of her curved and twisted, making Eleanor writhe like a cat in heat before him, unable to control her responses as her hips began to move of their own accord, meeting the thrust of his fingers.

"Very good wife." Edwin's voice was like the chocolate drink she had with breakfast, sinking into her with a melting heat and filling her belly with warmth. Every time his hand rubbed over a particularly tender spot on her bottom she shuddered and her body tightened around his fingers. "You like that it hurts, don't you? You just don't want to admit it."

She shook her head, not sure which statement she was responding to, but unwilling to trust her voice to answer. Everything had become confused.

There was a slight rustle of clothing behind her and then Edwin's fingers retreated, leaving her moaning for relief. It only took a moment before his hard rod was splitting her open from behind, bringing back the memory of the first time he'd taken her from behind after a spanking. Now, as then, her body responded with eagerness, despite the jolts of pain every time his furred groin pressed against the tender skin of her bottom. His body hair rasped and abraded the welts, and yet she couldn't stop herself from pushing back against him, spearing herself on his shaft. It pierced her body open, sensuous friction as it tunneled into her wet heat, the heavy grip on her hips helping him to control the long slow strokes he was taking in and out of her body.

Eleanor groaned and shuddered, wriggling as Edwin took his time with her, admiring the sight of her disciplined bottom jiggling as she tried to back herself onto him. The pink crinkled rosebud of her anus winked at him between her beaten cheeks, a sinful and delightful sight. Despite her obvious reluctance to show her arousal, honey was dripping from the hole he was thrusting into, coating his cock with a sheen of moisture. The punishment had not been pleasant, but the pain had easily been turned to erotic heat, giving way to rising pleasure.

From her movements beneath him, which were slowly becoming more frantic, he knew she was beginning to feel the crest of her climax. Her hands pressed into the bed, trying to push her body back against him to increase the pace of his thrusts, her hips wriggling in his hands. It took all of his self-control not to give in to the temptation to pound hard into her; instead he kept his slow, steady pace as Eleanor's erotic moans increased in intensity, rising in volume as her sheath tightened around him.

"Edwin... Edwin *please*..." The need for release was becoming

GOLDEN ANGEL

almost painful, her husband's control over her body, over the pace of their lovemaking was keeping her right on the edge of culmination without allowing her to go over.

"Tell me Eleanor," he leaned forward, driving deeper into her as she gasped, his voice hoarse with lust. "Tell me you like it." His hands shifted on her hips to cover her bottom, fingers digging into the soft, reddened flesh, awakening nerve endings with fiery tendrils of pain that blossomed and combined with her pleasure. Back arching she cried out, pushing back against him, wanting more of the exquisite mix of sensations he was creating within her, not caring where it came from. "Tell me, sweetheart."

"I like it," she sobbed out, pushing back against him. "Oh God Edwin... don't stop..."

He growled and lunged, slamming into her mercilessly, just the way she craved it. The abrading roughness of his thrusts against her bottom, the fast hard thrusts into her shuddering quim, sent her careening forward into a free fall of ecstasy. Eleanor writhed before him, beneath him, her sobs of pleasure falling onto his eager ears as she tightened and convulsed around his rampaging cock, moaning his name over and over again.

With a grunt of exertion, he pulled himself free of her body and grasped her around the waist, tossing her up fully onto the bed before she knew what was happening. His wife looked up at him with plea-sure glazed eyes, her body still trembling from the aftershocks of pleasure, as he crawled on top of her, sliding his cream-covered cock back into her snugly, squeezing passage.

"Edwin... oh no... It's too much..." Eleanor's eyes rolled back into her head as he thrust strongly into her, her body overwhelmed by the feel of her husband's weight on top of her, her sensitive bottom rubbing against the nubby material of the bed sheets in a way that sent sparkles of pain sizzling through her. Yet the overriding sensa-tion was one of extreme pleasure, pleasure so intense she struggled uselessly against it as her husband began to ride her again, filling her over and over as he rutted between her splayed thighs.

Her fingers dug into his shoulders, nails scoring over his muscles as she heaved and writhed beneath him. Legs wrapped around the backs of his thighs, Eleanor's body seemed to draw him deeper even as she pleaded with him to slow down. Mewling whimpers escaped her throat as her bottom flared with heat on the sheets beneath them, her insides quivering and tightening around the thrusting iron rod, her husband's flesh pulsing within her own.

"Again sweetheart," Edwin demanded, his voice rasping over her senses as he buried his face into her neck, biting at the sensitive skin. She gasped and undulated as his hand slid down between them, rubbing against the swollen, sensitized nub at the apex of her sex.

"No, Edwin, I can't... I can't.... oh please..." Eleanor's back bowed, so forcefully she almost lifted her husband off of her as he tormented her swollen flesh.

"Yes, again," he murmured, and bit her earlobe as he squeezed and thrust.

Tears leaked from her eyes due to the intensity of her climax, she screamed Edwin's name—a feat he'd never accomplished before no matter how pleasurable her prior releases had been. The sound of his wife wild with passion echoed in his ears as her legs and arms wrapped around him and held him tightly, every muscle in her body rigid and throbbing. He groaned and shuddered as he emptied himself into her hot cavern, filling her with jet after jet of creamy seed.

They rocked together, their movements slowing as their muscles unwound. Wrapped around each other so closely he could barely tell where he ended and she began, Edwin closed his eyes and greedily inhaled the scent of his well-pleasured wife. She was so soft and supple beneath him, everything he'd ever dreamed a wife would be. For this he would endure a great deal more than an evening without dinner.

When he finally released her, Eleanor let out another little whimper and rolled onto her stomach, easing the pressure off of her bottom.

Edwin chuckled as she let out a moan of relief now that the tender area wasn't being crushed by their combined weight.

"Stay here sweetheart," he murmured into her ear. For a moment

Eleanor hated him. As if it wasn't already humiliating enough that he'd punished her and then commenced with taking his marital rights, and doing it in such a manner that she'd lost complete control over her body, now he was laughing at her?

But she quickly revised her feelings towards him when he came back to the bed and began to smooth a cool cream onto the flaming globes of her bottom.

"Ooooooo... that feels so good..."

It was amazing how Edwin's hands could be hard as rock when he was spanking her as opposed to the gentleness with which he now touched her. There was a tenderness to the slow circles he made on her flaming skin, soothing her both physically and emotionally.

"I've been thinking sweetheart," he said conversationally and Eleanor bit back the immediate retort which sprang to her lips. "I'm going to neglect you terribly for the next three days and then we're going to go on our honeymoon. I think it's best if we get out of the city for a few weeks. We were both thrust into this so quickly, we'll be able to gain some distance from our day to day lives, spend some time with each other and then have a fresh start when we come back." Very gently he turned her over onto her back so he could see her face, slightly flushed and her eyes still a little swollen from crying while she was being punished, she looked absolutely beautiful with her disheveled blonde hair falling around her shoulders. "What do you think?"

"If it pleases you, Edwin," she murmured, making it sound as though she would agree to anything he wanted, although he was fairly certain he saw a small spark of excitement in her eyes. For some reason part of her didn't want him to know how wonderful that sounded to her.

"Shall we go to Paris, darling?" he asked, sliding his hand up her stomach to fondle her breast. Eleanor bit her lip and her eye lashes fluttered as her nipple darkened and hardened under his touch. Leaning his face closer to hers, Edwin brushed damp hair back from her forehead with his other hand. "Would that make you happy?"

"Yes," she whispered, and then bit her lip again, her expression looking almost confused.

It was a good idea, Edwin decided as he lowered his mouth to hers, kissing her gently at first and then with rising passion. Shifting on the bed so his long body lay against the length of hers, he continued to fondle her breasts as he deepened the kiss. Eleanor was fighting the marriage, but perhaps instead of familiarity what she really needed was a complete change of scenery to help her adjust. There were too many distractions from each other here; not just his work but their social lives, their friends... on their honeymoon she would have to interact with him and he could work at making her happy while simultaneously doing what he could to uncover the sweet and generous woman he knew she truly was.

CHAPTER 8

*T*he next three days passed quickly for both Edwin and
Eleanor as they readied for departure. His sudden
announcement had taken her by surprise and she found her time
filled with overseeing packing, sending their regrets to invitations and
the other million small duties that needed to be seen to in order for
travel. There was barely time for her to have a small chat with her
mother, most of which centered on the plans for Hugh's wedding. The
slightly bitter jealousy she'd been feeling every time she'd had to hear
about Hugh's wedding plans had mostly dissipated now that she had
her honeymoon to focus on.

Hugh was taking Miss Chandler on a honeymoon to one of the
family's many estates. As she was not at all well-traveled and hadn't
been anywhere but her own family's estates and London, Irene had
expressed herself content to stay within England. Since Hugh hated
to travel this suited him admirably; he much preferred to spend his
time out at the country estates with his horses and dogs, fishing and
comporting himself outdoors. In the few private moments brother
and sister stole together to converse, he expressed his excitement
about showing Miss Chandler the estates, as she'd declared herself
quite a country miss at heart.

An unsettled feeling had roiled in the pit of Eleanor's stomach as her brother enthused over how well matched he and Miss Chandler were. Somehow, from the few implications of her character he made, Eleanor's understanding of Miss Chandler did not seem to match her brother's at all. She had certainly not received the impression that Miss Chandler would prefer life in the country over the glitter of London Society, and the odd conversation she'd had at the dinner party with Irene stuck in her mind. But how to bring such a subject up to her brother? Before she could decide to speak, her mother interrupted their conversation and she and Hugh did not have another opportunity to speak.

Although she did not see Edwin during the day, he more than made up for his absence when he came to her rooms at night. Other than the days when she'd had her courses, Edwin had been a constant presence in her bedchamber, and these nights he seemed especially amorous. Her bottom was still quite sore, although healing, which only seemed to arouse him further. The very first evening he'd come into her bedchamber as Poppy had been brushing her hair. Dismissing the maid, Edwin had taken over the task. It had been a remarkably intimate experience, having her hair brushed by her husband, watching him in the mirror as he dragged the brush through the golden strands. With his broad shoulders and darkly handsome countenance he'd looked almost like a sinful dark angel, looming behind her light and gold features; dangerous yet erotic.

Soon he was dragging his fingers through her hair, rather than the brush, winding his hand into the silky locks and tipping her head back to devour her mouth in a hot kiss. They hadn't made it to the bed for that evening's first round of amorous pursuits. Instead Edwin had sat her upon the hard wood of her dresser, taking her away from the cushioned seat she'd been resting upon, and she'd cried out as he'd pounded into her, her sore bottom bouncing on the uncomfortable surface and somehow enhancing the pleasure she found as he speared her over and over again. Indeed, every night Edwin seemed to enjoy reawakening the soreness in her bottom, and to Eleanor's shame her climaxes were more intense than ever before.

Yet when he finally handed her up into their carriage to depart for the docks, Eleanor found her husband had considerately placed her favorite cushion upon her seat, to ensure she would ride in comfort. As they were leaving in the early morning she found herself leaning against her husband's broad shoulder, feeling strangely warm and secure beneath his arm. Neither of them were in the mood for conversation it seemed, and she drifted in and out of sleep as the carriage jolted and bounced along the streets, the slight chill of the morning air having no effect on her as she was warmed by her husband's body.

As usual her emotions towards her husband were conflicted. She still resented him for the loss of her Season, even though she knew that was as much her father's fault as Edwin's (and perhaps just a little bit of her own), and she hated how he had continued her father's methods of spanking... and yet the pleasures he brought to her body were so wondrous as to be unimaginable. Even when her bottom had burned their coupling had been intensely satisfying, even more so than usual. Edwin was a mass of contradictions—stern, gentle, punishing, caring... the welts on her bottom had healed much faster than ever before thanks to the cream he had rubbed onto it. Now he was cradling her as if she was something infinitely precious. It was all too easy to lean into him and drift away.

Strong arms wrapped around her and swung her up into the air. Blearily, Eleanor blinked her eyes and squirmed.

"Hold still," said Edwin, his voice sounding somewhat weary but also amused. "I'd hate to drop you in the water."

"I can walk," she said grumpily, but she curved her arm around his neck, holding tightly to him as she let her head drop back onto his shoulder.

Edwin nearly purred with satisfaction feeling her snuggling up to him again. The carriage ride had been immensely enjoyable. When Eleanor dropped her guard she was a wonderfully tactile creature, not at all the nagging harpy she occasionally made herself out to be. Perhaps knowing she would have an elaborate and romantic honeymoon, when their wedding had been anything but, had finally softened her to him. Although he hadn't seen much of her the past few days something had certainly changed in her demeanor. Perhaps it was the birching but perhaps it was the trip as well. Even Mrs. Hester hadn't had any complaints over Eleanor's conduct as his wife had thrown herself into settling everything within the household so they could leave.

Although it was now mid-morning he, like his wife, was feeling the effects of their hastily planned departure. Fortunately they hadn't had to plan their own dinner last night, they'd dined with Eleanor's family who had wanted to give them a send-off but would rather do so the evening before than the morning of. Edwin had received a note from his own family that afternoon, expressing regret that they had missed his wedding and imploring him to bring Eleanor to the Manse after they returned from their honeymoon. He had to grin and shake his head at his parents' foibles, the largest being their reluctance to leave the estate.

Laying Eleanor gently down onto the bed, he undressed her despite the fact she was only half-awake and tucked her in before divesting himself of his own clothing and crawling in beside her. His wife murmured sleepily and squirmed next to him, tucking herself into his body in the most delightful way. If they weren't so tired he would have taken advantage of their unclothed state, but part of their exhaustion stemmed from how late he'd kept them up the night before. Wrapping his arms possessively around her soft form, Edwin closed his eyes and, despite the erection which was cradled against her stomach, fell almost instantly asleep.

WHEN ELEANOR AWOKE, feeling completely refreshed, it was to the smell of the sea, the gentle rocking of the boat, and the shouts of the sailors. She immediately became aware of the large masculine body wrapped around her, something she was unused to as Edwin normally awoke well before her even when he slept in her room. It wasn't entirely unpleasant to feel the hard length of his body pressed against her back, his heavy limbs across her legs and stomach. One hand cupped her breast gently, fingers not quite gripping but curved over the soft mound possessively.

The hard ridge pressing into her bottom, which was only a little bit sore now, indicated she wouldn't need much effort to wake her husband and receive satisfaction, but she was too excited about her first time being on a ship. She wanted to walk the decks and see the ocean. Carefully she started to wriggle away from her husband's furnace of a body, squealing as his arm suddenly tightened around her and hauled her back.

"Where do you think you're going?" Edwin's dark eyes glinted with amusement as he turned her onto her back, his voice still fuzzy with sleep. Propping himself up on one elbow he cupped a breast in a gentle hand and toyed with it, rubbing his thumb over her nipple in a way that made her breath hitch.

"I was going to go up on deck," she said, staring up at him. "I want to see everything."

Her husband's eyes drifted down her body, which was uncovered to the waist, and Eleanor felt her cheeks heat. She didn't think she would ever become accustomed to the lasciviously proprietary way Edwin looked at her whenever she was unclothed. And often even when she was clothed. The little spark in his eyes always preceded a thorough bedding, to the point where every time she saw it, her pulse started to race.

"I like the view down here just fine," he said in a rasping growl.

"Edwin!" Eleanor half-laughed, half-protested in exasperation as her husband shifted his weight on top of her, trapping her lower body beneath his as he peppered small kisses along her jaw, trying to reach her mouth.

"Stop moving away," he complained.

"I just told you I want to go up on deck!"

"You'll get there a lot faster if you'd cooperate." The teasing, coaxing tone of his voice was that of a little boy's, reminiscent of when they were younger and he would tease her into doing some-thing they would invariably get into trouble for later. Only now there was no one to hold them accountable for what they were about to do except for her.

He'd ignored the push of her hands against his chest, using his legs to pin her down as he caressed her breasts. Although she tried to ignore the tingling sensations he was awakening in her body, she could feel herself losing her conviction to go above decks. After all, the ocean wasn't going anywhere. There would be plenty of time, and if she went up now she would be hot and aroused without the release she so enjoyed. She moaned, allowing Edwin to capture her lips as he squeezed one of her turgid nipples, toying with the sensitive bud, tugging at it as he coaxed her body to the state he desired.

Feeling her submission beneath him, Edwin deepened the kiss. Awakening with an armful of soft, warm woman trying to wriggle away from him had spurred his desires; although he didn't need immediate release upon awakening, feeling her trying to leave their bed had sparked an unusual amount of need in him. Eleanor writhed as he kissed down her neck, her hands rubbing over the flexing muscles of his back as he pleasured her. There was something satis-fying about having her acquiesce to him, knowing she had wanted to go above decks but he could rouse her body enough to change her mind.

Dragging his tongue across the soft satin of her skin, he groaned as her legs parted further, his cock nudging at the damp flesh of her sex as she opened to him. The urge to shove deeply into her and ride her was nearly overpowering but he beat it back. He would not start his honeymoon with a quick fuck; by the end of this trip he wanted Eleanor to be deeply content with their marriage and he was of the firm belief that keeping her satisfied in the bedroom would assist mightily with that. He had not forgotten her suggestion of separate households, a suggestion which still made him feel somewhat panicked. While he didn't expect miracles when it came to her atti-tude, indeed he would be fairly disappointed if she never needed another spanking, he did want her to accept him and to do her best to please him as he was doing his best to please her.

Sucking one rosy nipple into his mouth he slid his right hand between their bodies and teased the slick folds of her quim. Eleanor's breath caught on a small cry as she shuddered, her hips lifting to meet his fingers, her body demanding more pressure from him. Attending to each of her nipples in turn, wetting them with his tongue and biting down gently to roll them between his teeth, Edwin made small circles against her heated flesh with his fingers, never touching the little scrap of flesh that ached for him the most.

"Edwin... Edwin *please*..." Eleanor's back arched as her body twisted, trying to force Edwin's hand to caress her in the way she needed, to bring her to the brink and push her over.

With his weight supported on one hand, the other busily working between her thighs, Edwin leaned over her face so he could stare directly into the foggy sapphire crystal of her eyes. Her pupils were large and black as she whimpered through swollen lips; although her eyes were open he was quite sure she wasn't truly seeing him.

"Please what Eleanor," he asked, his breath wafting across her face, thumb stroking over the hood of her clitoris, just enough to make her jerk but not enough to bring her to orgasm. "Tell me what you need sweetheart."

"You... please... I need you inside me... Edwin... take me... *please*..."

This lust-crazed plea, combined with the raking of her nails down his chest, was more than he could have hoped for. His thumb thrummed across her clit, pressing down on the aching bud and rubbing hard enough that she shrieked, eye lashes fluttering madly as her body convulsed in ecstasy. Maneuvering himself quickly, he pressed his cock to her slick folds and impaled her with one hard thrust. Eleanor could barely breathe, her body was so overcome with sensation as she was split open in the middle of her climax, the pulsing rod sending her higher on a wave of sensual bliss.

Edwin rode her hard, knowing he wouldn't last long under the circumstances—he never did when he had just woken, which was why he'd pleasured Eleanor with his fingers first. He could feel his wife shuddering in continuous climax around him, her body in constant motion beneath his as she clung to his neck and sobbed his name. The passionate whimpers and groans that fell from her lips only spurred him to a faster, harder pace, the walls of her sheath sucking at him as she tightened and spasmed over and over again.

He groaned her name as he filled her to the brim, the dark hairs of his groin melding with her honey gold curls as the swollen folds of her sex were crushed against his body. Inside of her he pulsed, his body rubbing up and down so she continued to squeeze and massage his cock throughout his release; his body slowly relaxing atop of hers as spurt after spurt of hot fluid gushed into her tunnel.

With a sigh of satisfaction he kissed the sides of Eleanor's neck, feathering them along her jaw and cheeks until he reached her lips. She kissed him back so sweetly he thought he might melt on top of her. They cuddled in the afterglow, for the first time truly relaxed. Although he'd enjoyed their relations at home he'd always felt a bit rushed about the aftermath, knowing he needed his sleep so he could be up early the next morning to continue setting his affairs in order for their trip. Now they had all the time in the world for him to caress and kiss her, to bask in the warm afterglow.

For Eleanor this was absolute bliss. The way Edwin was looking at her made her feel cherished, something which she'd never experienced before. Her parents had loved her, of course, as had her brother, but nothing compared to this. Edwin was touching her as if she was made of glass, his eyes filled with a soft wonderment that made her feel like the most special, wonderful person in the world.

Perhaps she should stop fighting him. Despite the punishments Edwin had treated her very well—and she certainly had deserved some kind of retribution for the trick she'd pulled on him at the dinner party. It was not the marriage she would have chosen, but he didn't seem to expect her to jump at his command, unlike her father and mother. Nor did he worship at her feet, the way she might have wanted him to, but perhaps this new adoration she saw in his eyes... could it be enough? They had plenty in common, they knew each other well and they had passion. Perhaps she should just make the best of the situation.

"Would you like an escort to the deck?" Edwin asked, smiling down at her in a rakish manner which seemed to imply he'd be more than willing to keep her right where she was. In that moment she made her decision; they were on their honeymoon and she was going to give them a chance. They should rub along together well enough if she stopped instigating trouble.

"I would please," she said, as demurely as she could considering her husband was still inside of her. Reaching up she brushed a dark lock of hair from his forehead, and saw the pleased look in his eyes as she made the first small gesture of affection to him that she had since their wedding.

~

PARIS WAS GLORIOUS. The dresses, the freedom, the art, the people... Eleanor enjoyed the lighter restrictions on behavior. She and Edwin were able to sit at a private table for two even in a public restaurant, she could laugh as loudly and freely as she wanted without anyone staring, and the dresses the other women were wearing made hers look positively conservative. Not that she ever wore one without the fichu, but she could tease Edwin about buying a "real" French dress and enjoy listening to him growl possessively.

A kind of fond camaraderie grew between them as they walked the streets, watched the entertainments, attended the theater, and flirted at parties. Other women watched in envy as Edwin danced attendance upon his wife; Eleanor was not slow in noting that more than one of them tried to tempt him from her side. At first, she'd been shocked by her reaction—a blinding possessive jealousy which had rendered her nearly speechless as Edwin had smiled benignly at the glittering beauty and pretended not to know her meaning, keeping Eleanor's hand pressed tight against his forearm with his own hand.

"You are so attentive to your wife," the lady purred, managing to both glare at Eleanor and bat her eyes at Edwin. "The men here... they are not so devoted as you." The way she said it seemed to imply that Edwin's devotion only went so far as Eleanor's gaze. She gritted her teeth and opened her mouth, but Edwin gave her wrist a small pinch and she closed her lips as he answered the hussy.

"Perhaps they are not so lucky as to have a wife such as mine," he said smoothly. The lady frowned and blinked. The words themselves were almost an insult, and yet there was nothing about Edwin's manner or tone implied it was so. Eleanor nearly laughed at the other woman's consternation, even as a warmth filled her. She looked up at Edwin just as he was looking down at her and their gazes caught and held. All the jealous bile seemed to drain out of her as she basked in the glow of her husband's attention.

The French lady muttered something under her breath about newlyweds and love and stalked away.

At first, she'd worried over her reaction, and then she decided it was only natural. Certainly it wasn't love. After all, she had decided to make the best out of her marriage with Edwin, it was understandable she would have a feeling of possessiveness about him now that she had accepted him as her husband. Besides it was a point of pride with her, proof of her desirability, to keep him from straying. Especially considering they were on their honeymoon. The brazenness of the women was almost insulting to her.

However, possibly the most shocking revelation was when men flirted with her in Edwin's presence. Not only did she find herself unattracted to any of them, despite the fact that many of them were quite handsome, but Edwin's demeanor changed drastically as he went from simply standing next to her to somehow actually *looming* beside her and radiating an unwelcoming coldness to the gentlemen. There was a dangerous air to him when she was first approached by any unknown gentleman, usually almost immediately followed by a return to their hotel—and once with a passionate tryst in their hosts' conservatory. The closest Eleanor had come to such illicit behavior had been receiving a kiss at her come-out ball, certainly not the kind of heart-pounding amorousness combined with the edge of anxiety which came from engaging in intimacies in such a public avenue.

For himself, Edwin was pleased to watch Eleanor blossom, although he could have done without other men noticing her golden beauty and the sweet joy she took in life. She attracted men like honey attracted flies, and yet now she wasn't trying to attract attention she seemed entirely unaware of her conquests. The other women in the room didn't hold a candle to her and they seemed to know it; although it didn't stop them from trying to compete with her for his attention. Not one of them appealed to him as much as Eleanor; they didn't have the complexities of her character or the inner, unjaded innocence she exuded. Back in London he'd worried she'd lost that inner light, but away from her family and acquaintances, seeming to have accepted their relationship, it was shining brightly again. He never wanted to see her grow hard and cynical like her friend Lady Grace and the Eleanor he was seeing now in Paris didn't seem in any danger of doing so. It was almost like she was a completely different person; an adult version of the Eleanor he'd known as a child, no longer the hardened socialite with a mission.

One afternoon Eleanor went shopping while Edwin entertained himself at one of the gentleman's clubs. He'd given her a budget this time of course, but had issued no commands or warnings about the kind of purchases he'd like her to make, which she greatly appreciated. It seemed he trusted her now, after the past two weeks in each other's company, and she found she relished having his confidence. Now that she was no longer fighting it, marriage to Edwin had become quite... enjoyable. Her decision to become an amiable wife seemed justified; he now seemed inclined to let her do as she wished.

After selecting three gowns that were daring but elegant, quite fashion forward and she was certain would be all the rage in London, Eleanor found herself being distracted by the modiste who, upon discovering Eleanor was newly-wed, insisted on showing her some nightgowns. At first Eleanor had resisted, although she hadn't wanted to explain that her husband preferred she wear nothing at all to bed, but then the modiste seemed to realize what Eleanor was implying.

"*Non, non,*" the woman said, laughing gaily as she waved away Eleanor's vague explanations. "These will not be for *sleeping*. Trust me, *cherie*, your husband will appreciate *these* nightgowns."

When Eleanor glimpsed the fabric of the gowns she understood. Some were silky, some were sheer, others had lace appliques in strategic positions... her favorite was a silky gown of palest pink that caressed her skin as it was slipped over her head. The fabric clung like a second skin, the skirt swirling around her legs as she moved before settling back around her curves. The paleness of the color made her skin creamier, her hair more golden, and emphasized the natural pink of her lips.

Staring at herself in the mirror, recognizing the kind of temptation this sweetly, innocently seductive gown would have on Edwin, Eleanor ran her hands down her sides. She felt like a completely sensual creature in this gown; the silk caressed her sides as well as her hands, and she immediately wondered what Edwin's reaction would be to touching her through this kind of silk.

"I'll take it."

"Bon! Very good, I thought so," said Madame, smiling cheerfully. "Try another, yes?"

Eleanor agreed immediately. In the end she bought three negligees, as Madame called them. Remembering Edwin's reaction to the red dress at home, how he'd wanted her to wear it only for him, she thought he wouldn't mind the purchase. She got the silk pink one, of course, and another sweetly innocent one made of white with inserts of chiffon in the skirt so as she walked and the skirt flared her bare legs flashed teasingly. The third one was made of a completely sheer dark violet fabric with clever lace appliques over the breasts and in a band around her hips. While she wasn't certain whether or not she would have the courage to wear such a daring garment, even with Edwin as the only audience, she couldn't resist.

She was able to take the nightgowns home with her, with the rest of the dresses to be delivered to the hotel the day after tomorrow. Happily humming a popular waltz to herself, Eleanor practically danced out of the shop on feet that felt lighter than air.

THAT NIGHT when Edwin came into the bedroom Eleanor was there, pretending to a calm she didn't feel. This was the first time she would truly be initiating intimacies between them. While she had teased and flirted with him often enough and occasionally kissed him since they'd begun their honeymoon, she had never done so in their bedroom. Tonight, however, she knew she was waving a red flag in front of a bull with her attire.

In the soft flickering light of the fire and the candelabra by their bed her skin almost seemed to glow next to the iridescent sheen of the pink silk.

Edwin strolled in with his usual air of eagerness, his fingers already busily untying his cravat, as he threw a smile full of sinful promise her way. His head turned away for a mere moment before snapping back in a most satisfying manner, arrested by the sight of her standing next to the bed in her new nightrail, her fingers already gently resting on top of it. Frozen, he stared at her, greedily drinking in the sight, committing it to memory.

The eagerness with which he always approached their bedtime was overrun by a burning need to claim, to possess. The trepidation on Eleanor's beautiful face gave way to thrilled triumph, her body slowly shifting from a rather anxious stance to a sensual languor that only increased his ardor.

"Eleanor..." he rasped, his voice feeling tight in his throat, the air in his lungs burning. "What on earth are you wearing?"

"Do you like it?" she asked, slowly twirling as she lifted up her arms, the silk shifting and sliding over the soft curves of her body. A small smile lifted her lips when she heard her husband groan as he was treated to a spectacular view of the way it hugged her backside.

She let out a squeal as she found herself lifted; Edwin had rushed her from behind, overcome by the need to touch her. Tossed onto the bed, she twisted around to see her husband practically tearing off his clothing in his hurry to join her. Anticipation sparkling in her clear blue eyes, she lounged backwards, enjoying the effect every movement she made had on him. The ever suave former rake was struggling with his clothing, unable to tear his eyes away from her as he continued to disrobe, revealing the hard planes of his body so many women in Paris desired to see and touch.

And he was hers, all hers.

Practically purring Eleanor got onto her knees and crawled across the mattress towards him. Arrested by the sight, Edwin paused for a moment, his breeches only halfway down his legs as he stared at her.

"You didn't tell me whether or not you like it," she murmured, settling on the edge of the bed, her weight on one elbow as she stretched out her legs along the side of the bed.

Finally naked, Edwin reached out and traced his hand down the side of her body, making her catch her breath as her skin heated beneath his touch. Beneath the silk her nipples hardened in anticipation, rubbing against the wonderful fabric.

"You look... I don't have the words for it," he said in a husky voice, his eyes following the movement of his hand as it traced its way down to her thigh. "Like temptation. Like innocence. Like half of my fantasies come to life."

Eleanor pouted at him teasingly, pushing herself up onto one hand. "Only half?"

Something in his eyes glinted wickedly. "Would you like to see the other half?"

Curiosity welled as she stared up at her husband, looming over her, magnificent in his nakedness. The musculature of his body was caressed by the dim lighting, he was completely unabashed standing before her, his manhood proudly erect and so hard it practically touched his stomach. Reaching out she caressed the steely length, amazed—as always—by the velvety softness of his skin sheathed over iron. Edwin shuddered and groaned, his head falling back for a moment as her slim fingers wrapped around him.

As much as he wanted to grab her and have his way with her, he was enjoying her new brazenness. He wanted to see how far she would go in her explorations. Although she'd touched him before, had taken his cock in her hand, it had almost always been at his behest and encouragement. She had certainly never blatantly displayed herself the way she was now—she'd never needed to. Edwin needed nothing more than to think of having his wife and his blood would begin to pound. This new side of her that she was showing deserved to be encouraged, to be developed, so he didn't want to rush past it.

Although, if she did want to indulge in his fantasies then he would be taking control away from her immediately anyway, but he wanted it to be her decision.

Sliding her hand up and down Edwin's length a few times, pumping him in her tight grip, Eleanor was entranced by her husband's reactions. His jaw and fists clenched, as if every part of him was holding back. The power she had over him in this moment was enthralling.

But she wanted to know her husband's fantasies, and she knew she couldn't possibly match him for expertise in sensual matters. While she hated to think of how his knowledge had been gained, hated to think of him doing this with any other woman, she comforted herself with his apparent singular interest in her bed. If she knew his fantasies, if she learned from him all that he knew, then she could keep him from straying. And if he did, then she could use her knowledge to repay him in kind, with any lover of her choice. But she didn't consider that an option for now, what she desired were ways to tie Edwin to herself.

She'd already come to terms with the knowledge that she wouldn't have quite the marriage she wanted. As much as Edwin desired her, he never spoke in words of love or treated her the way she'd imagined her husband would, but it was obvious he desired her and she could gain much of what she'd originally wanted from a besotted husband through a husband that desired her. It seemed to her that the more she could please him in this arena, the happier her marriage would be.

Some small part of her in the back of her mind seemed to say she was making excuses, thinking of convoluted reasons to hide her desire to please Edwin, but she ignored that. Trying to please her husband didn't mean she would end up like her mother, after all, Edwin was obviously trying to please her as well and he was doing a very good job of it. It was only natural she reciprocate.

"Show me," she said, cutting off any further chance for thought, wanting to sink into the delightful physicality of their passion, knowing that doing so would make further introspection impossible.

Edwin opened his eyes again, their dark depths smoldering with a fire she was becoming very familiar with. He reached for her...

Less than thirty seconds later Eleanor found herself in a very familiar and very unwelcome position.

"Edwin!" she protested as she struggled to get up from her position over his lap, his forearm easily holding her in place.

"Relax sweetheart, this is for pleasure, not for punishment."

"Whose pleasure?" she asked sarcastically, although she had to admit to herself that the way his hand was caressing her bottom through the silk nightgown did in fact feel quite nice.

"Not all spankings have to be unpleasant," he said, and his hand came down sharply on her bottom.

Sharply but not painfully. Eleanor jumped at the contact, more indignant than anything else. It didn't hurt, no, but she wasn't entirely pleased at this turn of events. The first time he had spanked her over his lap she'd been unwillingly aroused by his nearness, by the intimacy of it. Now, over his naked lap, she was more aware than ever of the heat of his body, the press of his cock against her side. There was no doubt her husband found punishing her bottom arousing, but she hadn't realized it would feature in a fantasy, she thought they'd do something new.

"I love seeing your pretty bottom turn pink," Edwin said, lifting the hem of her skirt up so he could see the creamy globes, caressing and then spanking again. Eleanor blushed to hear him speak so indelicately, somewhat shocked at his admission. She hadn't been unaware that disciplining her had an effect on him, but she had certainly never expected to hear him express such a sentiment. The hand on her bottom lingered after each sharp bite, as if he was rubbing the slap into her skin, but instead of increasing the pain the caresses somehow turned the pain into something else. Something hot and wanton, not quite pleasure, because it still hurt, but something that wasn't punishment at all.

Burying her face in the bed she muffled her whimpering moans as he slapped and caressed, all too aware of the excited increase in his breathing, the hardness of his manhood pressing against her body.

Her own sensual heat was rising along with the temperature of her bottom. Edwin had been nothing but truthful when he'd said not all spankings were the same. This one was a wholly new experience for her, the biting smacks and the firm press of his fingers rubbing against her skin as the silky night gown slipped and slid against her body was arousing her to an almost painful degree.

When his hand dipped down to press between her legs, Edwin found his wife was sopping wet, her curls soaked with honey. A throaty cry fell from her lips as he thrust two fingers into the ready aperture, penetrating her swollen heat. He nearly groaned as he felt her flex around his fingers, pumping the digits back and forth in her clasping hole for several strokes before pulling them out and sucking the juices from his fingers. Eleanor writhed on his lap, a vision of golden hair and ivory skin, the pale rose of her bottom matching the delicate pink of her nightgown. She had submitted completely to him, allowing him to indulge in his fantasy without protest, responding to it with all the ardor he could have wished for.

SLAP!

His hand came down on her upturned bottom again, and he gripped her flesh harder this time, digging in his fingers a bit and enjoying the way she writhed on his lap. "Do you like it Eleanor?"

SLAP!

Gasp. A low moan. Fingers pushed inside of her and then pulled out as she tried to move her hips back to catch them. SLAP!

"I can feel how hot and wet you are." The masculine growl in Edwin's voice was becoming deeper, almost threatening. "I want to hear you say it, Nell."

SLAP!

She flexed her fingers in the sheets, feeling almost dizzy with the overload of sensations as his fingers delved her depths again, craving the sensation of being filled. Was she silent because she didn't want to answer or because she didn't want him to stop? Eleanor wasn't sure.

SLAP!

Edwin's hand came down across the swollen lips of her sex, the strike reverberating through her center as she arched her back and let

120

out a cry that was half-protest, half-ecstasy. It stung, it burned... and it felt so good. Her insides clenched and pulsed emptily, hungering, wanting.

"Edwin..."

"Tell me," he insisted, rubbing his fingers over her pouting flesh, cleverly avoiding the erect bud of her pearl, circling his fingers around it and teasing her senses. She felt nearly mindless from the wash of sensations coursing through her.

"I want you," she whispered, almost shyly, turning her head just slightly to peek at him through the falling locks of her hair. He wasn't looking at her face; his eyes were greedily, hungrily drinking in the sight of her bottom as he ran his hand over the warm flesh, before bringing it down hard again. For the first time she saw his face as he spanked her, the hot, hard expression on his face, the eagerness in his eyes, the way his tongue flicked over his lower lip as if he was tempted to somehow taste her reaction.

"That's not what I asked, Nell," he said, and now he did turn his head towards her face and she quickly turned hers away, her cheeks blushing hot pink, as if she'd been caught doing something illicit. There was something feverish in her husband's dark eyes, making them glow with faint embers, like charred logs in a dying fire.

For a moment she was silent, feeling Edwin's long fingers caressing her warmed bottom, sliding down over the wet curls around her sex, trailing along the crease between her buttocks and her thighs, and then returning to curve over the pink globes in a proprietary manner.

"I like it." Although her voice was soft, it wasn't quite a whisper, more of a confession, a thread of wonderment in her voice at her admission. "Not... I don't like it when you spank me to punish me. But I like this." Shyly she peered over her shoulder again, meeting Edwin's eyes. There was a strangeness to the expression on his face, something she hadn't seen before. As if her words had affected him more deeply than he'd anticipated.

The intensity of electricity between them seemed too much to bear and he tore his gaze away, returning it to her exposed bottom.

Raising his hand he let loose a flurry of spanks on her vulnerable cheeks, giving vent to some of the emotion constricting his chest. Her cries of pain and pleasure as she jerked and shuddered over his lap did the same for Eleanor, submerging these new feelings into over-whelming physical sensation.

Then she was turning—or rather, being turned—and she found herself on her back, Edwin tugging the silky nightdress from her body. Willingly she raised her arms and let him bare her completely. The soreness of the skin across her bottom was filled with a sensual heat; he hadn't spanked her long enough or hard enough for it to truly hurt, only enough to ignite the fires of her passion, the part of her inner desires that responded to being spanked by him.

He scooped up his cravat from the floor and grasped her wrists, deftly winding the fabric around them as Eleanor blinked with surprise, completely taken aback.

"What—?" Eleanor started to ask, blinking her startled blue eyes as Edwin lifted her arms above her head, forcing her to lie down on her back with her hands almost pressing against the headboard.

"This is part of my fantasy," he murmured into her neck, his fingers deftly tying the cravat around one of the posts in the headboard. Eleanor's soft body beneath him was shivering with excitement, her hard nipples rubbing against the wiry hairs of his chest, and he was exerting every ounce of his willpower not to just thrust into her and take her immediately. But he wanted to enjoy this moment, to indulge his senses, and drag this experience out for as long as possible, especially now that she was bound and completely vulnerable to him.

Part of her thought she should have been frightened, her hands twitched as she realized she was securely restrained and couldn't move her arms at all, but instead she found her excitement rising as she began to breath faster. Anxiety rose along with her anticipation as Edwin raised himself up on his forearms to look down at her, as if she was a tasty treat he was going to devour. She'd often thought he looked like a dangerous predator, so darkly masculine with a potent air of power to his movements, but now she realized she also trusted him. Strange... how could she trust a man who had taken a birch to her unwilling backside? Who had brokered a marriage deal with her father behind her back and not even allowed her half a Season? And yet, now that she was completely helpless before him, beneath him, she realized she did trust him at least enough not to be frightened even though she was at his mercy.

Edwin didn't miss the trepidation on his wife's face or the lack of real fear in her eyes; she was unsure of what his intentions were but she was not afraid of him. The surge to take her, possess her, claim her, was rising higher than ever before. This honeymoon they'd taken had done more than helped them to settle into their marriage, it had strengthened the bond that had already existed between them to a degree he had never thought possible. Looking down at her like this, her cheeks becomingly flushed, eyes glowing as if lit from within, with her peaked nipples and supple, ready body, he knew he would never get enough of having her in his bed, in his life. The time spent together had uncovered the young woman he'd thought must have been there, the sweet, friendly girl she'd been when she was younger, only in an older and much more appealing package.

Was she the reason he had never considered marriage before? Was it possible he had been waiting for her all these years and hadn't even known it?

Lowering himself on top of her, Edwin captured her lips with a kiss, plundering her mouth as his hands ran down her vulnerable sides. He could feel her shiver beneath him as the helplessness of her situation was reconfirmed as she automatically moved to embrace him, her bound wrists tugging uselessly. Moaning into his mouth, Eleanor's body undulated beneath him as sensual excitement ran through her. They'd spent more than enough time in bed for her to know exactly how pleasurable it could be, and she could sense there was a new urgency to Edwin's caresses, a new kind of anticipation in the taut lines of his body. Having her bound beneath him was exciting them both.

Somehow it made the sensations even more intense as he began to kiss his way down her body, her sensitive neck and collarbone, his hands cupping and kneading her breasts. She could do nothing but moan and lay submissively, accepting his touch, unable to reciprocate. When he began to suckle at her nipples she cried out, his teeth were biting into the tender flesh almost painfully and yet her back arched, thrusting her chest upwards as if begging for more. The rosy bud jutted out wet and proud when he pulled his mouth away, a darker pink than its counterpart due to his ministrations, and he moved his mouth to the other, biting and sucking just as hard as his fingers tormented the previous object of his affections.

"Edwin pleeeeeeeeeease," Eleanor keened, her hips lifting and pushing against his hard body as he tugged and twisted one nipple, nipping and sucking almost brutally hard on the other. "Be more gentle..."

The nipple popped from his mouth and he rested his elbows on either side of her, pinching both nipples between his fingers to tug and roll them, not at all gently, as he looked down into Eleanor's eyes as her body squirmed beneath his. "Are you telling me you don't like it? That your sweet little quim won't be soaking wet if I touch it right now?"

Eleanor closed her eyes against his scrutiny, whimpering in the back of her throat. The truth was that even when it hurt she was aroused by his rough handling, the same way she responded when he spanked her or even when he'd birched her.

"That's what I thought," Edwin chuckled as he pinched her nipples even more tightly, making her cry out as a flash of exquisite pain went through her straight to her core. The little buds throbbed when he finally released them, and Eleanor opened her eyes to see her husband grabbing one of their pillows before moving further down her body. When he spread her legs wide open, much further than she had done so herself, she blushed hotly as he stared at her splayed sex, knowing he was seeing the evidence of her arousal. On her chest her nipples were like ripe berries, a dark pink color from the abuse they'd taken, and yet she wanted nothing more than for Edwin to fill her up and bring them both to pleasure.

"Lift your bottom," he said in a husky voice, his eyes trained on the bounty of wet, hot female flesh before him. Obediently Eleanor planted her feet on the bed and pushed upwards, lifting her hips so he could slide the pillow beneath her. The pillow kept her raised from the bed, allowing Edwin easy access to her hot slit.

Lowering his head, he slid his tongue straight up the center of her womanhood, his tongue flicking against her woman's pearl when he reached the apex. Eleanor cried out and writhed as he pleasured her with his tongue. Normally she enjoyed using her hands to press his head further into her flesh, to help her rub herself against his lips and tongue; now she had no control over the sensations rippling through her and that just aroused her even more.

Edwin's hands and arms slid under her thighs, lifting her up even more as she spread her legs wider, his fingers searching out her breasts and aching nipples. They were sore, but the tugging jabs of pain that went through them as he began to toy with the tender buds again only heightened the pleasure. Eleanor gave herself over to the sensations, the exquisite blend of pain and ecstasy Edwin was so skilled at creating within her. Her hands tugged at the cravat, loving the way her bound wrists increased her excitement as she pulled helplessly.

"Edwin... oh Edwin...!" she cried out as her body tightened, clenching down as she threw her head back and rubbed her hips up and down against him. Her husband sucked the swollen nub of her clitoris into his mouth, pulling on it with his lips as she shuddered with orgasmic bliss against him. The heady smell of her musk filled his nostrils, the taste of her honey coating his mouth.

The movements of Eleanor's body began to change as the rapture became so intense it began to hurt, her muscles almost cramping they were wound so tightly and she thrashed against her bondage. "Edwin please! Stop... it's too much... oh God... I can't.... Edwin *please!*"

But he ignored her, releasing her breasts from his hands to bring them down and curl his arms around her thighs, his shoulders beneath them and his hands wrapped around to the sensitive inner part of her legs, pulling them apart as she tried to press them together in an attempt to force him away from her throbbing flesh. Eleanor begged as she convulsed, Edwin's tongue laving torturously and lovingly over her overstimulated clit, his hands forcibly holding her wide open for the oral assault. There was nothing she could do to stop him and she screamed as she careened wildly off of a cliff of pure physical sensation, driven by a much stronger orgasm than she'd experienced the first time.

As she sobbed and pulled at her wrists, Edwin thought his cock might actually explode. It was the most beautiful thing he'd ever seen. He loved having Eleanor laid out helpless before him as he feasted upon her, knowing she was totally at his mercy and within his power. Knowing he could lavish pleasure on her until she was literally begging him to stop. This was like a banquet for his senses, and he intended to sup his fill.

As she came down from her second climax, Edwin released her legs. Already wrung out from her useless struggles and the intense orgasms, Eleanor's eyes were closed, her muscles lax as Edwin arranged himself over her. She let out a little whimper as he rubbed the head of his cock up and down her slit, shuddering but not truly moving as he circled her clit with the blunt tip.

"So beautiful," Edwin murmured as Eleanor finally opened her eyes and looked up at him. Tears were still gathered on her lashes, her cheeks flushed and bright, eyes foggy with the haze of sensual bliss. Grasping her hips in his hands, he held her pressed downwards, her body lifted to the perfect angle by the pillow beneath her, and began to push into her hot, tight tunnel.

Eleanor moaned and shuddered as Edwin entered her, stretching her open so deliciously and yet... could she truly take anymore? Her husband had bound her, licked her to one orgasm and then forced her to a second, and now she felt as though her limbs were weighted, all of the strength gone from them, and she felt sure he would not be satisfied until she was crying out in ecstasy beneath him again. Not once, during their entire marriage, had Edwin taken his own pleasure until she had done so. But right now Eleanor wasn't sure she wanted to again, even though having Edwin inside of her felt absolutely wonderful, her outer parts felt swollen and abraded from so much stimulation.

Looking down at his wife, Edwin could see the consternation on her face as he thrust in and out of her helpless body, the flashes of pleasure and discomfort as he rubbed his groin against her swollen folds. The pillow had tipped her up perfectly, allowing him deep access to her tunnel, so he could plunder her fully. The small convulsions in her body, the way her insides tightened around his cock as he seated himself deep inside of her, all spoke of her body's readiness to climax again with the proper encouragement. Yet he knew she must be close to her breaking point. No longer struggling against the bondage around her wrists or the ardor of his body, she looked anxious as her own body began to respond to the thorough fucking he was giving her.

Releasing her hips, Edwin leaned forward and took her mouth in a kiss, changing the angle of his body so it pressed against her clit with every thrust. Eleanor's cries of protest were muffled by his lips as she jerked beneath him. Wrapping his arms around her back, he clasped her closely, fiercely, as he began a rapid assault on her tender opening, splitting her over and over again with strong thrusts that rubbed his body against her. Eleanor's legs thrashed on either side of him, thighs trying to press together but unable to withstand the much stronger force of his hips moving into her, taking her with all of the pent up lust he'd been holding back.

She wailed, her mouth breaking free from his, as she was forced into her strongest orgasm yet. Her breath sobbed in her throat as her body spasmed, her tunnel gripping him, practically strangling his cock. Feeling her come apart beneath him, Edwin let loose the last of his passion, pumping strongly as he took her, claimed her. With a low cry he poured himself into her, the hot seed being sucked from his cock into her eager sheath.

With her eyes closed, Eleanor went limp beneath him as he half-collapsed on top of her, feeling her chest rise and fall as she sucked in great breaths of air. Reluctant to divest himself of the warmth of her body, Edwin balanced himself on his elbows and snuggled his head into her neck. With her pulse slowly returning to normal, Eleanor turned her head to cradle him there.

CHAPTER 9

$\mathcal{E}$leanor sighed as they pulled up in front of the London House, looking out of the carriage window a little mournfully at the Mayfair house where she and Edwin lived. They'd enjoyed their honeymoon so much they'd ended up extending it until they absolutely needed to return in order to be present at Hugh and Miss Chandler's wedding.

A little squeeze of Edwin's fingers around her hand got her attention and she turned to look at her husband, every inch the English gentleman, seated next to her and gazing at her with a soft look in his eyes.

"I wish we could have stayed in Paris as well," he said, smiling at her, and she knew he'd heard her sigh.

"It will be good to see everyone," Eleanor replied, putting the best face on their return home. "And Mama would never forgive us if we missed Hugh's wedding."

"I'm not sure Hugh would forgive me either," said Edwin with a chuckle. Eleanor laughed. Considering he was Hugh's best man, she knew her brother would have been quite upset if they had stayed on the Continent.

Still, she mused as Edwin handed her down from the carriage, she couldn't help but feeling as though a time of magic was over. Now they were back in the world they truly inhabited... would they remain the same, as a married couple, as they had been on their honeymoon? Or would things go back to the way they had been before?

"I'm sure Mrs. Hester will be happy to see us home, especially you," said Edwin as he led her up the stairs. There wasn't any censure in his voice, but she was quite sure he was referencing the fact that she hadn't taken up her duties as his wife within the household the way she should have before they'd left for their honeymoon.

"Yes," she replied dutifully. Neglecting her responsibilities to their household had been one of the many ways she'd used to rebel against the marriage she hadn't wanted, but she hadn't forgotten her decision to make the best of the marriage while they were on their honeymoon. That would continue now that they'd returned, and she was willing and ready to assume the mantle of Edwin's wife and do her best to make their marriage work. "I'm sure she'll be relieved to no longer be responsible for the entire household."

Edwin smiled at her as they entered the front door, obviously pleased at her easy acquiesce to his hint. She smiled back, warmth blooming in her chest at his approval. Strange how a little more than a month ago she felt resentful at his approval and now she craved it.

"Edwin! Eleanor!"

Both of them turned in surprise to see Hugh and Wesley hurrying towards them from the receiving room, where they had obviously been waiting for the couple to return. Hugh was as handsome as ever, his face glowing with excitement—as it should be with his wedding a mere week away—his golden hair swept back in a new style, and his blue eyes set off by his navy coat and cobalt waistcoat. He swept his sister up in a hug and twirled her around as she laughed over his exuberance, hugging him back with excitement.

When he set her down they were facing Wesley and Edwin, who were clapping each other on the back and exclaiming over how well the other looked. In truth, if Wesley had not been with Hugh, she wasn't sure she would have recognized him. His time in India had bronzed his skin and lightened his brown hair, bringing out tints of gold and coppery red in the long strands. Unfashionably long strands, tied back at the nape of his neck, and yet it suited him. Dressed in full mourning black for his father, Wesley looked rather dangerous, both rugged and somehow refined, and she was sure his reappearance in Society had sent many young women swooning.

"Little Nell," he said, shaking his head as he reached for her, pulling her into his arms for a swift hug. Eleanor hugged him back, shooting a swift glance at Edwin to see he did not mind, but he was grinning and greeting Hugh.

"Not so little anymore," she retorted as she pulled away.

Wesley rolled his bright hazel eyes, his unrelenting grin softening the hard lines of his face, his teeth gleaming whitely in his bronzed visage. "Not at all, and married to Edwin of all people! I thought you had better taste than that."

To her surprise Eleanor was able to laugh without feeling any stab of disgruntlement over her lack of choice in a groom. The time away with Edwin had obviously done wonders to help her come to terms with the wedding.

Pulling a resigned face she shook her head. "You should have seen the empty headed ninnies he was dancing with at the balls, I couldn't possibly have left him to such a fate."

"But that's the fate you've left me to," protested Wesley, one hand over his heart as he pretended to feel faint. Edwin and Hugh were laughing at their friend's antics, he had always been the joker of the group. "How shall I endure?" He moaned and lay one hand dramatically across his brow before shooting her an inquiring glance. "Unless of course, you have a friend in mind for me?"

"None that would suit," she said honestly, grinning up at him. "I'm afraid you're on your own."

"Cruel woman, not even a hint of apology in her," said Wesley shaking his head.

"You have no idea how hard it is to encourage her to apologize," said Edwin with a chuckle and Eleanor flushed bright red.

"My condolences on the passing of your father," she said hastily to Wesley. It abruptly sobered the conversation as Edwin added his own condolences, which she did regret, but the words needed to be said and she certainly preferred it over listening to Edwin make references to disciplining her. Wesley accepted the sentiment with a little grimace, she knew he and his father hadn't been particularly close but there was still a shadow over his face.

"Would you like to have a drink?" Edwin asked, shooting a little glance at Eleanor and she smiled and gave him a nod. Although they'd just returned home she certainly didn't mind that he wanted a moment to catch up with his friends, especially Wesley who had been gone for so long. And it would give her the chance to find Mrs. Hester and begin to find out what exactly she needed to do around the house. Wesley and Edwin continued to chat as they went down the hallway towards his study, leaving her momentarily in the foyer with her brother.

"You look happy Nell," said Hugh after they'd studied each other for a moment, a slight expression of relief on his face. Eleanor couldn't help but smile; even though she knew Hugh looked at her with the often exasperated eyes of a henpecked big brother and thought Edwin could do no wrong, he'd obviously been worried about a mismatch with the way things had been going after their wedding. "Did you enjoy your honeymoon?"

"Are you supposed to want to know about things like that?" she asked, innocently batting her eyelashes.

"Nell!"

She laughed and stepped forward to put her hand on his arm. "I find myself content, Hugh. Now go along and play with your friends, I have things I need to see to around the home."

"More than content," Hugh said with a certain amount of surprise at her desire to attend to her responsibilities (which made her bristle a little even if he had reason to be surprised by such a turn of events), followed by a smugness on behalf of Edwin. Grinning, Hugh gave his baby sister a kiss on the forehead, suddenly well satisfied that things within this household were well in hand and no interference on his behalf was needed. "You're the very picture of a happy woman in love Nell."

And with that he turned on his heel and strode down the hallway, blithely oblivious to how he'd just brought his sister's world crashing down around her ears.

Stunned, Eleanor stared after her brother, his words echoing in her ears, pushing at her with their weight and threatening to smother her. She couldn't breathe. She couldn't see. She couldn't think.

The very picture of a woman in love.

A woman in love.

A woman in love.

Oh merciful... how could this have happened? The revelation slammed into her so hard she felt faint, as if the floor had dropped open beneath her feet and the curtains drawn back to show her the truth behind her behavior for the past month. When they were in Paris she'd let down the barriers she'd built, hoping to find a way for them to coexist happily. Contentedly. Amiably.

Instead she had fallen in love with her husband.

In love with a man who was very much like her father with his heavy hand and disciplined attitude, with his unbending will and strength of character. In love with a man who was nothing like the man she'd planned to marry, who had already had her dancing to his tune and deciding to desist in her own aims before she'd even realized her feelings towards him, a man who had given no indication that he suffered from such an affliction himself.

While she was sure he cared for her in his own way, after all they had practically grown up together, it wasn't the same as the feelings she now realized she had for him. And he desired her. For now. Yet she knew that was not enough to sustain a marriage, not in their world. How long before even his desire for her mellowed and he began to look for a bit on the side? How could a man like him possibly be satisfied with just one woman for the rest of his life without love to bind him to her? She would spend the rest of her life trying to please him, because she loved him, and he would treat her with a distant affection until she became a shadow of herself, idling away in the country and ignoring whatever pursuits her husband might be indulging in whilst in town.

Eleanor's feet were moving before she could think, running, taking her to the refuge of her chambers, although she couldn't outrun the fact that her greatest fear was coming true: she was turning into her mother.

∾

IN HIS STUDY, Edwin poured three glasses of port and handed one to Wesley, keeping one in hand and settling the third on the table next to the empty armchair for Hugh once he joined them.

"To happy reunions," he said grinning as he raised his glass. Wesley laughed and raised his hand as well before taking a sip of the port.

"Very nice," said Wesley approvingly with a sigh as he settled back into his chair. "You'd be amazed how hard it can be to get a glass of good port in India."

"What was it like?" Edwin asked, curious. There were many changes in his friend, not the least of which was a seriousness to him Edwin had never seen before. He wondered if the changes came from Wesley's travels or from the burden of his new title as the Earl of Spencer.

As Wesley told him of the dry dusty land, the monsoon season and the colorful fabrics and people, Hugh joined them and settled down to his own glass of port, looking rather content. Edwin was a little curious about what Hugh and Eleanor had spoken of, but he was too enthralled by the tale Wesley was weaving around them to divert the conversation just yet. He spoke of the hard-eyed, brown-skinned swordsmen, the sharp division of the classes, the elephants and monkeys, and the very strangeness of the culture in comparison to their own.

"And the women..." Wesley said, a sudden grin flashing across his face as his eyes unfocused in a rather nostalgic expression. "You wouldn't believe the attention the Indians put into their amorous pursuits."

"Oh really?" asked Hugh, leaning forward with interest. Edwin only smiled. He was quite happy with his own amorous pursuits and didn't particularly feel the need for embellishment. For a moment he let his mind wander back to Paris, where Eleanor had allowed him to spank her for pleasure several more times; once he'd even turned her bottom a hot cherry red as she'd whimpered and even cried a little, but hadn't asked him to stop. In fact their love making had been even more intensely passionate than ever. Not that she would admit she liked being spanked, and he certainly didn't indulge every time, but the occasional one allowed him to get the itch out of his hand.

Shifting uncomfortably in his chair, Edwin pushed his mind back to the conversation at hand where Wesley describing some of the sexual positions the Indians had invented and their various drawbacks and rewards. As well as some of the "extras" they used.

"In fact," said Wesley with a twinkle in his eye. "I brought home presents." He turned to Edwin. "I brought yours and handed it over to Banks in case we didn't see you today."

"And where's mine?" Hugh demanded in mock indignation.

"It will be your wedding present," retorted Wesley as Edwin rang for Banks. "I missed Edwin's wedding so he gets his now." It was only a few minutes before the butler returned with the package Wesley had brought, a box tied neatly in packing and filled with straw to cushion its contents.

"What is all this?" Edwin asked curiously as Wesley pulled out several bottles.

"This one," Wesley held up a large green bottle with a black stopper, "is massage oil. It enhances the experience admirably." He held up another bottle. "This one is for ah... lubrication."

"I'm not sure I need that one." Edwin grinned wickedly.

"I didn't hear that," Hugh muttered as he picked up the massage oil to examine it, a thoughtful look on his face.

"It might not be what you think it's for," countered Wesley, grinning wickedly. Edwin raised an eyebrow at him as Hugh looked up, confused. "Gentlemen, there's a whole world of pleasure out there we have missed out on. Things that are acceptable in other cities would require us going to some of the worst, most degenerate dens of iniquity in this city."

"Such as?"

"Have you ever enjoyed a woman's bumhole?"

Edwin shook his head and Hugh just laughed.

"Are you saying some woman actually let you put your cock in her arse?" asked Hugh, still laughing. "You actually expect us to believe that?"

The white flashing grin on Wesley's face said he didn't care whether they did or not. "And she enjoyed it. The lubrication helps. As do these." He pulled out a smaller box and opened it, revealing four objects of increasing size.

"Those are dilators," said Edwin, reaching out to touch one of the hard rubber things. "I saw an advertisement for them in the paper, they're to relieve constipation."

"Which I'm sure they do, but they're also quite useful for stretching a woman's rosebud to a point where she can accommodate a man. They're all the rage in ah... certain places."

Edwin ran his finger over the hard rubber of the smallest dilator, it wasn't much thicker than his finger and he had a sudden vision of Eleanor on her hands and knees, bottom in the air as he pushed this strange thing inside of that forbidden orifice. The image caused a wave of lust which nearly brought him to his knees and he eyed the box with new interest. Although he was quite content with things as they had become while he and Eleanor were in Paris, there could certainly be no harm in exploring new vistas of sensuality.

"And if the woman doesn't like it, and happens to be a willful spoiled brat, they're rather useful for discipline." Wesley eyed Edwin, but out of respect for Hugh (who grimaced) didn't go further into specifics. The image in Edwin's mind changed to an Eleanor with bright red buns and a plugged anus, and he coughed a little as he tried to get a control of his wayward libido.

"What are these?" he asked, hastily opening another little box in order to change the focus of the conversation. Inside were what looked like earrings, but with the kind of screw clamps he'd seen used by carpenters, only in miniature.

"These beauties are to adorn a woman's nipples," said Wesley, taking them from Edwin and deftly demonstrating how to adjust the tension of the prongs with the tiny screws. Both Hugh and Edwin were utterly fascinated, both imagining them on very different feminine forms. "They will pinch, and the tighter they are the more they pinch and the less time you can leave them on." Edwin had to squash the urge to run upstairs and try them out immediately on his wife. Considering how much she enjoyed being spanked, even if she never admitted it and claimed only to be doing so because it was his fantasy, he was sure that adding a little bite to another sensitive part of her body would result in the same kind of passion.

"What's in this?" asked Hugh, picking up the smallest, and last, bottle in the box.

"That, my friend, is a very powerful aphrodisiac. Three drops with your wine in the evening and make sure you have the entire night to indulge yourself or you'll regret it."

Both Edwin and Hugh studied their friend, to see if he was joking, but there wasn't even the slightest hint of mirth on Wesley's face. A little bit of ruefulness and a hint of nostalgia, but it was obvious he wasn't having one over on them.

The last thing in the box was a book, which Wesley said was called the Kama Sutra and contained over a hundred sexual positions, all with their own name. Edwin decided he would look at it later, in private or with Eleanor, and the men returned to their seats.

"I'm surprised you're in London, actually, although I'm glad to see you," said Edwin to Wesley. "But I thought you would be out at Hammersby." Hammersby was Wesley's main estate now, the seat of his earldom and where the rest of his family spent most of their time.

Wesley shuddered. "I was there long enough to get things in order, but believe me, an escape back to London was necessary."

"Your mother?" Edwin guessed, thinking Lady Spencer had probably taken immediate advantage of her son's presence to begin encouraging him to do his duty as Earl—which to a mother's mind always involved marriage.

"Shockingly no," Wesley said. "Mother is in Bath with my father's, well I suppose she's my ward now. My brothers, on the other hand, are both at Hammersby and they are pestering the daylights out of me.

Matthew wants me to buy him a commission, he's gone completely army mad, and Vincent wants me to send him to some school in Italy where he can study art of all things." Wesley tossed back the rest of his port in exasperation as both Hugh and Edwin chuckled and Edwin refilled the glass. "Of course Father had turned them down and Mother is completely against Matthew going into the army. Vincent claims she was coming around on his desire to travel, if not his choice of studies.

But they want me to give them permission and funds to pursue their 'dreams' while she's away dealing with Cynthia, leaving me to face the music when she finally returns and finds out what I've done."

Both Hugh and Edwin burst out laughing at the look of resigned consternation on Wesley's face. They knew he would do exactly that in the end, and his brothers probably did too. Considering he had traveled his own path, managing to travel as he pleased through his own ingenuity and in defiance of his father's wishes, he would not stifle his brothers now that they were of a similar age as to when he'd set off. But he obviously didn't want to be left alone to deal with his mother's recriminations either.

"Cynthia's your ward?" Hugh asked.

"Yes, I haven't actually met her yet. Mother took her to Bath to slowly introduce her into Society." He hesitated. "Matthew said she's very pretty but a little wild... apparently Mother thought she might do better away from the influence of my brothers and in the company of other young ladies."

"I can only imagine what trouble your brothers might have encouraged her to get into," said Edwin, grinning. "Do you remember how often we talked Eleanor into doing things we were too scared to?"

Hugh laughed. "Like the time she stole the chocolate tarts we were supposed to have for dessert that night? She would have gotten away with it too if she hadn't gone back for seconds."

"Which she only did because Edwin wanted another one," Wesley teased, a smile creeping over his face as they fell into reminiscing rather than talking about his current difficulties.

"And she never told on us either," Edwin said shaking his head, thinking ruefully about Eleanor's somewhat misplaced loyalties towards the three of them when they were younger. She'd always been tagging along behind them wanting to join in with whatever they were doing. Perhaps Wesley's ward was experiencing something similar with his brothers. "How old is your ward?"

"Cynthia? Ah..."

"He doesn't know!" Hugh chortled. "What a terrible guardian you are!"

"I've had a rather lot on my mind," Wesley said in exasperation. "My mother mentioned it to me but there have been more pressing matters to remember than some schoolgirl chit's age. She's close to coming out."

"So she must be nearing seventeen or eighteen," mused Hugh. "I wonder if your mother wasn't worried about a completely different kind of trouble from your brothers. Matthew's what, twenty-two? Vincent is nineteen? And Matthew said she was pretty."

Wesley frowned, considering, and Edwin felt a little pang for his friend. Two years ago Wesley would have found that kind of situation to be something of a joke, he would have preferred to think his brothers were enamored rather than just leading a young miss into trouble and would have been the first to place wagers on which of his brothers would steal a kiss from the chit first, or if his mother would be a stalwart enough chaperon to keep them at bay. Either the responsibilities of his position or lessons learned when he traveled had obviously steadied him and given him a more serious outlook on life; he was obviously taking the responsibility of a ward more seriously than Edwin would have guessed. He and Hugh exchanged glances, but Hugh just shrugged and smiled a little, as if to say this new more pensive side of Wesley was something he'd already become acquainted with and was no longer unexpected to him.

"I suppose I'll have to check into that too," Wesley muttered. He sighed and rubbed at his forehead.

Out of the three of them, Edwin knew Wesley had been the least prepared to take up the reigns of the Earldom. Hugh's father had begun handing over certain responsibilities to Hugh when he was only twenty-four, making sure he was familiar with every inch of the estate and the duties which came with it. Because Edwin's parents abhorred the city, his father had begun sending Edwin in to take care of business as soon as it became feasible, knowing Edwin rather enjoyed time in London. In contrast, Wesley's father had been a rather overbearing man who had difficulty giving up any kind of control, basically demanding Wesley learn the knowledge without ever taking an actual hand in running things. For someone of Wesley's active nature it had been paramount to torture and he'd left rather than stayed and learn under his father's looming tutelage.

"Your mother seems to have it well enough in hand, if she's taken the chit to Bath," Edwin said consolingly. "And it might not be the case anyhow."

"I hope not. Matthew didn't seem as though he was pining for her and neither did Vincent." Wesley mused a bit more and then relaxed, his familiar grin spreading across his face as he looked back at Edwin. "Enough about me. How's married life? I have to admit, I always thought Hugh would be wearing the ball and chain before either of us."

Hugh sputtered a little and shot Wesley a look, but there wasn't much he could say in his defense. He had been the first of them to start noticing girls as something more than a nuisance and he'd certainly been the most romantically inclined. Neither Edwin nor Wesley had ever been inclined to remember things like a girl's birthday or her favorite color, and although they'd certainly used flowers and such as gifts neither had taken any particular notice of what kind or color of flowers they were sending. In fact, the only woman Edwin had ever paid such attention to was Eleanor and that was because... well because she was Eleanor. She'd always been a breed apart to him.

"Ha, look at that smile," laughed Wesley. Edwin started a bit with surprise, realizing he hadn't actually answered his friend. "You look like a cat that got into the cream."

"No details please," muttered Hugh. Lounging in the armchair like a blonde Adonis, nothing in his manner gave away any discomfort they were discussing his sister and Edwin's relations with her, but that didn't mean he would remain so amiable if Edwin started spouting off things he didn't want to hear.

"Well then that should answer your question," Edwin retorted. "Married life is quite agreeing with me at the moment, although at first I'd had my doubts."

"Hugh said Eleanor wasn't exactly thrilled with the arrangements at the beginning." Wesley chuckled, but his tone was questioning. As it should be, they'd all known Eleanor long enough to know she didn't like anyone arranging her life.

"I think she's settled down now," said Edwin. He grinned suddenly. "A few spankings and a trip to Paris did wonders for her attitude. We had a marvelous time. I think she's realized being married to me isn't so bad after all." Although he hadn't quite meant to his voice took on a rather salacious and masculinely smug tone any other rake would recognize, much less his friends.

"You spank her?"

"Of course," said Edwin. "I had to birch her before we left for Paris… she held a dinner and purposefully chose a menu that practically ensured I didn't want to eat a bite of it."

Wesley burst out laughing. "God, who would have thought she'd do something like that? Ingenious. I'm sorry I missed it."

"I wish I had." Edwin was smiling though, he was no longer angry over the incident and he could certainly see the humor in it. Even admire her ingenuity a little now that it was past and she'd been duly disciplined for it. He knew she ended up truly regretting it. "Afterwards, I decided we should go on our honeymoon immediately, take some time to get to know each other again. I haven't had to spank her since. Although," his tone dropped conspiratially, "that doesn't mean I haven't."

"No details," Hugh muttered again.

"I can't believe little Nell is all grown up and married," Wesley said shaking his head, ignoring Hugh. "It seems like just yesterday she was tagging along behind us, demanding we join her tea party." He sent Edwin a sidelong glance. "Although she always had been more interested in your company than mine or Hugh's."

"Was she?" Edwin couldn't hide the surprise in his voice.

"Of course," Hugh said rolling his eyes. "Growing up it was Edwin this and Edwin that."

"You never told me that."

"You never noticed all the times we left you to entertain her and made our escape?" Hugh and Wesley exchanged grins as Edwin frowned, casting his mind back.

He supposed he had noticed, sort of. But he'd never felt as though he'd been ditched by his friends, on the contrary he'd often been quite content to share in Eleanor's adventures. Not having any siblings of his own it had been a wonderful new experience to indulge a little girl on occasion—and since he wasn't her real brother he hadn't felt any of the frustration with her that Hugh often had.

"Worked out well for me," he said rather smugly, thinking of how she'd turned into a beautiful, passionate young woman. He eyed the box Wesley had brought for him. Hugh looked at it, but rather than following Edwin's thoughts to his sister, Hugh's thoughts obviously went to his own bride and he let out an impatient little sigh. Edwin grinned. "Only a week to go Hugh and then you'll have your own bride well in hand."

"It can't come soon enough," said Hugh rather morosely, shifting in his seat. The movements of a man who hadn't been with a woman since he'd begun seriously courting.

"That was definitely one advantage of a quick wedding," Edwin muttered, and then raised his voice as Hugh shot him a look. Wesley covered his smile with a quick sip of port. "How is Miss Chandler?"

"Quite well," Hugh smiled as his eyes unfocused, the lines of his face softening and Wesley and Edwin exchanged amused glances.

"Have you met her?" Edwin asked Wesley.

"Very briefly. She seems like a well-bred kind of lady," said Wesley.

His tone wasn't condemning exactly, but it didn't seem entirely approving either and Hugh scowled at him.

"*Exactly* the kind of lady I want," said Hugh. "No matter how much Edwin might enjoy spanking my sister, I certainly don't want to spend all my time disciplining my wife." He shook his head at his friend. "I don't see the appeal at all. I'd much rather have a sweet, loving wife who doesn't cause me any trouble."

"Just like your mother?" teased Wesley.

"Better her than Eleanor," Hugh retorted. "I got quite enough practice having to dole out her punishments. I'll do so when needed with my wife, but it's not something I want to have to do on a regular basis."

"It's a very different prospect punishing a wife than a sister," murmured Edwin.

"How would you know, you don't have any sisters."

Wesley raised his hand. "I have to agree with Edwin. There's an entirely different element when you're spanking a lady you're sexually attracted to. Or birching her." He grinned and turned his head towards Edwin. "Have you tried a riding crop?"

"No details!"

"Now that's an idea."

"Does that mean you're planning on spanking your wife?" Hugh asked Wesley in an obvious ploy to turn the conversation to something else.

He snorted. "I'll not be taking a wife anytime soon."

"But when you do," Hugh persisted.

"Doubtful. That's not what wives are for. I'll have a wife for the heirs and a mistress for the spankings," Wesley said grinning. "I can't imagine too many well-bred English wives actually enjoying a good bottom warming." He looked curiously at Edwin who grinned and winked. Hugh heroically pretended not to see this exchange. Wesley sighed. "And the only one who might have is already married."

"Don't make me pour this on you," Hugh said, threatening Wesley with the glass of port in his hand. Edwin snorted and reflected he was very glad Wesley was home. Things just hadn't been the same without him.

As the other two exchanged various threats and insults, Edwin let his mind turn to his wife and he wondered how she was settling into the household upstairs. In another quarter of an hour he would join her and see what he could do to help. Perhaps they could browse through the book Wesley had brought.

UPSTAIRS ON HER BED, Eleanor took deep breaths, slowly calming herself. When she had first walked in the door she had been resigned to Hugh and Wesley taking Edwin's attention away from her for the first time since they had left on their honeymoon. Now she was grateful for it. Who knew what Edwin might have done if he'd seen how upset she'd become, what he might have guessed.

Staring blindly out her window, Eleanor told herself this wasn't a complete disaster. After all, Edwin didn't know she was in love with him. He had no idea the power he had over her. And perhaps he did have deeper feelings for her.

She would just have to test him and find out.

And if he did not then she could go back to her original plan and become such an inconvenience he wouldn't want to live in the same household as her. The very thought of being separated from him made her feel empty and nauseous, but surely that was better than losing herself to this chaotic surge of emotions, better than ending up like her mother. She would not be shunted off to the country at Edwin's whim, she would *choose* to go.

But only if he didn't love her.

Drying the tears from her eyes, Eleanor forced herself to calmness and began to plan how she would discover her husband's feelings.

EPILOGUE

*H*er hands shook as she dragged the brush through her hair, a shining gleam of ivory in the candlelight against the fiery tresses. Staring at herself in the mirror she felt as if she were looking at a stranger.

I can't do this.

It was far past the time she should have already been in bed and asleep. Her mother had sent her to her room hours ago to ensure she would be well rested for tomorrow's events. Just thinking about it unsteadied her breathing and sent her heart racing. At first she'd tried to sleep, she truly had, but after laying in the darkness with her thoughts surrounding her, unable to diminish her fears, she'd relit the candles and sat down at her dressing table. What else could a woman in her position do?

It wasn't as if she could shimmy out the window and run away.

Where would she go? Maybe… No. He wouldn't be able to help her. Even if he wanted to. She had no money of her own. Although she'd made friends during her Seasons, none of them would help her. Not with this.

"Irene?" The disapproving tones of her mother's voice made her wince as the bedroom door opened. "Why aren't you sleeping? You're going to have dark circles under your eyes on your wedding day!" The way she said it, dark circles sounded like the most tragic thing that could happen.

"I can't sleep," she said, setting the brush down and staring at the reflection in the mirror. Her mother entered behind her, wrapped in a comfortable looking blue robe, the cotton hem of her nightgown peeking out from the bottom. Looking at her, Irene realized she was slightly chilled, her own thin cotton gown not allowing much for warmth. "Mother... I... I'm not sure..."

The baroness sighed, coming to stand behind Irene and meeting her eyes in the mirror. Hard agate met pleading emerald without sympathy. "We've talked about this, Irene. You must marry Viscount Petersham." Her hand came to rest on Irene's shoulder, fingers digging into the soft flesh and Irene flinched. "We have no choice. You must marry someone who can take care of our debts and the only one willing to do so with the dowry of your land is the viscount. If you do not marry him we will be impoverished. And he seems to have some affection for you."

"That just makes it worse!" Irene protested, driven to it despite the hardness of her mother's expression and words. "When it was nothing but a business arrangement... what if he becomes angry with me for deceiving him?"

Her mother snorted. "I said he has affection for you, you foolish girl. That means nothing over time. Enough affection and he will get an heir and a spare on you quickly and then you can do as you please. He will have his own lovers, perhaps mistresses. It is the way things are done."

But what about love? Irene wanted to ask, but she didn't. She already knew her mother's views on the subject. But her mother could see it in her expression anyway.

Leaning down, her mother whispered in her ear, her hard, dark eyes trapping Irene's in the mirror. "When you have given him his children, he will have done his duty and have no more need for your bed. And then you may see if Lord Brooke returns your... affections.

But do not come crying to me if he uses you and your *love*," she said the word mockingly, "and then breaks your heart."

Irene didn't respond. She just sat, staring blankly into the mirror, seeing nothing. Regretting the day she'd unburdened her innermost thoughts about marriage and love to her mother. Wishing that she were anyone but the daughter of an impoverished baron. Hugh was a good man, she was sure of it. He didn't deserve a wife who was in love with someone else.

But what else could she do?

Did you enjoy this introduction into the world of Edwin, Eleanor, Hugh, and Wesley? The story continues in Dealing with Discipline *the second book in the series, a full-length novel continuing their stories.*

∼

DID you enjoy Birching His Bride? Would you like to receive a free story from me? Join the Angel Legion and sign up for my newsletter! You'll immediately receive a free story from my Stronghold series in a welcome message, and as part of the Angel Legion you'll also receive one newsletter a month with teasers, sneak peeks, and news about upcoming releases, as well as what I'm reading now!

PLEASE DON'T FORGET to leave a review!!! It's the nicest thing you can do for an author!

ABOUT THE AUTHOR

About me? Right... I'm a writer, I should be able to do that, right?

I'm a happily married young woman and I like tater tots, small fuzzy animals, naming my plants, hiking, reading, writing, sexy time, naked time, shirtless o'clock, anything sparkly or shiny, and weirding people out with my OCD food habits.

I believe in Happy Endings. And fairies. And Santa Claus. Because without a little magic, what's the point of living?

I write because I must. I live in several different worlds at any given moment. And I wouldn't have it any other way.

I also write erotica, fetish romance, and dark offerings under the pen name Sinistre Ange.

Want to know more about my other books and stories? Sign up for my newsletter! Come visit my website! I also update my blog at least a couple times a month.

You can also come hang out with me on Facebook in my private Facebook group!

Thank you so much for reading, I hope you enjoyed the story... and don't forget, the best thing you can do in return for any author is to leave them feedback!

Stay sassy.

www.goldenangelromance.com

facebook.com/GoldenAngelAuthor

twitter.com/GoldeniAngel

instagram.com/goldeniangel

OTHER TITLES BY GOLDEN ANGEL

Sci-fi Romance

Mated on Hades

Daddy Doms

Super Daddies: A Naughty Nerdy Romantic Comedy Anthology

Victorian Romance

Marriage Training

Domestic Discipline Quartet

Birching His Bride

Dealing With Discipline

Punishing His Ward

Claiming His Wife

Bridal Discipline Series

Philip's Rules

Undisciplined (Book 1.5)

Gabrielle's Discipline

Lydia's Penance

Benedict's Commands

Arabella's Taming

Venus Rising Quartet

The Venus School

Venus Aspiring

Venus Desiring

Venus Transcendent

Stronghold Series

Stronghold

Taming the Tease

On His Knees (book 2.5)

Mastering Lexie

Pieces of Stronghold (book 3.5)

Breaking the Chain

Bound to the Past

Stripping the Sub

Tempting the Domme

Hardcore Vanilla

Masters of the Castle

Masters of the Castle: Witness Protection Program Box Set

Tsenturion Masters with Lee Savino

Alien Captive

Alien Tribute

Big Bad Bunnies Series

Chasing His Bunny

Chasing His Squirrel

Chasing His Puma

Chasing His Polar Bear

Chasing His Honey Badger

Night of the Wild Stags – A standalone Reverse Harem romance set in the Big Bad Bunnies World

Poker Loser Trilogy

Forced Bet

Back in the Game

Winning Hand

Poker Loser Trilogy Bundle (3 books in 1!)

Made in the USA
Monee, IL
27 May 2021